THE
STRANGER
IN THE
WOODS

a CRIMSON FALLS novella
KIERSTEN MODGLIN

KIERSTEN MODGLIN

Love. Lies. Alibis.

Editing by: Three Owls Editing
Cover Design by: Alora Kate with Cover Kraze
Formatting by: Tadpole Designs

*For the fans—old and new—for supporting this crazy dreamer
in the land of crazy dreams.*

ABOUT CRIMSON FALLS

The worst place to be in early October is the town of Crimson Falls.

In the late 1800's, two brothers stumbled upon an unnamed village, surrounded by thick forest and fresh water to keep them protected and alive. The brothers were cruel men who wanted a home to call their own. In their darkest hour, the brothers slaughtered the villagers, dumping their bodies over the waterfall at the edge of town. People say the water ran red for weeks, giving the town its terrible name.

Ever since that horrible anniversary, Crimson Falls is haunted by its past with a present filled with violence and danger. Every October is filled with fear...and for good reason. On October 13th, the dreaded Founders Day, all the town's crime comes to a head. And by the 14th, fewer will be alive than before.

Crimson Falls is a fictional town, created and shared by 8 mystery, suspense, and thriller authors. Each novella paints a picture about life in Crimson Falls and the insanity that takes place leading up to Founders Day.

Do you dare to read them all?

2018

CHAPTER ONE

PRESENT DAY

W hen asked to describe her success in one word, Arlie Montgomery had chosen *ironic*. The interviewer had thought she was being funny, and so she'd laughed along, but in reality it *was* ironic. All of it. Her entire life had been ironic, but especially her career. For six years, Arlie had worked, unsuccessfully, as an author, trying every new marketing tactic to garner a buzz for her thrillers. She did book tours where a handful of enthusiastic people might show up. She kept her social media up to date. She read books to perfect her craft. She scrutinized every single plot point.

But, in the end, it hadn't worked. No one wanted to read thrillers from a female; her publisher had continually suggested re-releasing the books and all future works under a pen name. Again, it was ironic, because if she'd listened, if she'd chosen to use a pen name, the very thing that had catapulted her career to its greatest height would've done nothing for AJ Montgomery.

Of course, the most ironic part was that the greatest

success of her life, the thing she'd longed for for years, the thing she'd sworn over and over she would do *anything* for, was only made possible by the greatest tragedy of her life.

Growing up in a town like Crimson Falls, Arlie had always been obsessed with horror stories, thrillers, and suspense. It fascinated her, especially when things worse than the movies she watched and books she read were happening in her hometown. She was desensitized to the terror of it all at a young age. Where most children were scared, Arlie was fascinated.

So, when she married Brett, a man from a town a few miles north, Arlie convinced him to move to the town she'd always called home, and he'd agreed. Most of the time, Crimson Falls was just like any other town. They had festivals and schools and town hall meetings and a big Christmas tree lighting in December. But October, specifically the week surrounding Founders Day, was different. In a town that so many believed to be cursed by its ancestors, Founders Day was never a cause for celebration. Instead, it was a day where the crime rate grew higher every year. People knew some wouldn't make it to the next day. Citizens would die, they'd be robbed and attacked, all because of the curse. *The curse.* Arlie had watched and read enough horror to know that rumors of a curse, rather than any actual curse, were enough to do the damage she'd seen done. After all, at the end of the day, the crimes were committed by people. People were always the ones to fear. There was nothing supernatural about October thirteenth, just evil people using it as an excuse to be their worst selves.

On the day of her husband's death, a death that made

2

national news, a man named Norman Gates—*again, ironic, right?*— came into Brett's office building in the next town over with a gun. He killed four people before going after her husband's assistant. Brett stepped in, saving her life and ultimately stopping Norman from killing the hundreds of others in the building, but he was murdered in the struggle. He'd been made into a national hero. People from all over the world had written her letters and attended his funeral. For a while, he was mentioned daily on every major news channel, and so, of course, was his widow: Arlie Montgomery.

It only took a few Google searches of her name for people to realize she was an author, and so, success eventually ensued. People became fascinated with Arlie, wanting to know all they could about her life and, as a result, her books. It was instant. Overnight, she'd become a bestseller. Her books were getting mentioned every place she could hope for, and the money had begun to pour in. There couldn't have been a better time, as she struggled to make ends meet until her husband's life insurance hit. And though it was all she'd ever dreamed of, in the midst of a tragedy, none of the success seemed to matter. Her publisher was thrilled, her agent elated. All at once, the world seemed to know her name, and it seemed to be forgotten that she was still a grieving woman who'd lost the love of her life.

While he was alive, Brett had been her biggest champion, pushing her to write more, believing in her while release after release tanked. If he could've seen her, she knew he'd be so proud. But she would've given it all up, been a struggling author for the rest of her life, just to have him back. Brett was what mattered, and the clouded vision of chasing her dreams had let her forget that.

So, that day, as she approached the two-year anniversary of her loss, Arlie drove the quiet outskirts of Crimson Falls. Grief was quiet. Lonely. Success in a field that was primarily done alone was also mind-numbingly seclusive. So, surrounded by sadness and horror, and expected to write about both as if they weren't her entire life, Arlie sometimes needed the escape that came with leaving her town and driving around in silence. Pretending for a moment that she was on her way home to Brett. That he'd be waiting with glass of wine and supper, ready to hear about her day.

Like the year before, as she approached the anniversary of his death, Arlie was forced to reflect on all that had changed in her life since that horrible day. In truth, everything had changed. Everything and nothing. She was still in the same house. She still wore the same perfume. She still made coffee in the morning and ate a piece of chocolate every night. Her life, the routine of it all, was unchanged. But nothing was the same. Brett was gone. She was more alone than she'd ever been. She had more money than she could ever have dreamed of. The only book she'd released since Brett's death, the one she'd written in her last days with him, not knowing they were the last days, was an instant success. She had, by all standards, made it. She was regarded as the town celebrity. She had everything she ever wanted, but she would never feel that way. The tragedy outweighed any triumph, and she could never think about her happiness without being held down by the guilt she felt for the way her success had come about.

She slammed on her brakes. Staring out into the foggy woods, out of the corner of her eye, she saw something shimmering in the distance. Was it just a trick of light? It was hard to see anything in the shadowy woods, but her headlights were definitely bouncing off something on the overcast day. Was it a sign? A piece of trash? A person? It moved, and she slowed the car down further, watching. It was a person; she could tell as she drove a bit closer. Someone standing off in the field, a reflective vest on. She wasn't sure why she chose to stop because everything in her screamed that she should keep moving, but she couldn't. The man stood by the tree line, still several yards from her, watching. He wasn't moving, just staring into space as if in a trance.

"Are you okay?" she shouted, rolling down her window.

She wasn't sure if he'd heard her at first, though he turned to look at her slowly. After a few seconds of facing her direction, she watched his outline head her way. She should've felt fear, but it was only curiosity in her gut until he reached her car. His face and clothes were filthy, covered in dust, but his piercing eyes burned into her. He didn't speak right away, just stood there, staring at her with a strange, empty expression.

"Hello," she said, keeping her finger hovering over the button in case she needed to roll the window up suddenly. "Are you okay?"

"Who are you?" he asked, his voice gravelly as if he needed to cough.

"I'm...I'm Arlie. Are you from Crimson Falls?" They were on the outskirts of the town, still a good thirty miles from the nearest surrounding city, so she assumed he

5

must be. But in a town the size of Crimson Falls, any unfamiliar face like his was far from common.

He shook his head. "I don't know."

"What do you mean you don't know?" she asked, sensing his ominous tone.

He touched his temple as if in pain, turning his head so she could see the blood that stretched across his scalp and cascaded down over his ear. "I...I woke up out there. Where did you say I am?"

"Well, you're near Crimson Falls," she said, feeling skeptical. "But, I've never seen you around here before. Are you hurt?"

He touched his forehead where the wound was and winced. "I must've hit my head. How far to the nearest hospital?"

"Thirty minutes away, at least. The closest one is in Arbordale. I can take you to see Doctor Phillips, though. He's fantastic. He can at least look you over and make sure you're...you know, not dying."

He scowled at her. "Gee, thanks."

"Climb in," she said. "It's not far."

He hesitated, looking into her car. "I don't know..."

"Oh, come on, I'm hardly dangerous to you. I'm trying to be a good citizen."

"How do you know I'm not dangerous?" he asked, his question making her skin crawl. Before she could change her mind, he pulled open the door and climbed in the car. She glanced at the wound again. It was a long, dark gash from his upper left temple to the tip of his ear, a small piece of skin from his scalp hung loosely like a flap. It was a wonder he was alive.

"That looks really bad. I'm not sure how you're conscious right now."

He winced, flipping down the mirror and looking at the cut while breathing through gritted teeth. "I kind of wish I wasn't."

"What do you do?" she asked, putting the car in drive and heading for the town's limit. "Some kind of construction?"

He looked down at his clothes, pulling the vest out and staring down at its reflective tape. "Yeah, I guess so." Aside from the vest, he was dressed in jeans and a T-shirt, not what she assumed would be typical clothes for a laborer, but what did she know? Brett was never a hard labor kind of guy.

"You guess so?"

"I don't remember," he said, his voice suddenly sounding agitated. "I honestly don't remember anything."

"You don't remember anything at all? Your name? Where you're from?"

"Nothing," he confirmed. "Guess I took one hell of a pounding to the head, huh?"

She nodded, gripping the wheel tighter. Suddenly, she was nervous. What had she been thinking, picking up a stranger? For all she knew, this man was planning to hurt her or steal her car. Her gaze fell to her purse quickly, where her black leather wallet could be seen easily. He flipped the mirror closed. "Do you have a napkin or something? I'm getting blood on your seat."

"In the console," she said with a sharp nod. He lifted the lid, pulling out a napkin and holding it to his head with a sharp inhale.

"Ouch," he said stiffly.

"You're probably going to need stitches." She glanced his way. "Dr. Phillips may end up sending you to Arbordale anyway."

He groaned. "As long as he can give me some pain meds, I'll be fine. God, this hurts, and I can't seem to get it to stop bleeding." He paused, looking at the napkin. "Thank you, by the way. For picking me up. I have no idea how I ended up out there."

"You're welcome," she said, surprised by his sudden politeness. "So, you really don't remember anything?"

He shook his head. "It's...fuzzy. I feel like it's right there," he touched a place on the opposite side of his head, "but I just can't reach it. It'll come back, though, I'm sure." He looked her way. "Right?"

She nodded, her jaw tight. "Of course. Sure, it will."

CHAPTER TWO

A rlie led the stranger into Doctor Phillips' office, a small, Southern home in downtown Crimson Falls. "Good morning, Miss Roberta," she greeted the receptionist.

"Good morning, Arlie," she said. "How are you today? Did you have an appointment?"

"No," Arlie answered. "We have a bit of an emergency."

"Oh my," Roberta said, standing up as she saw the man and noticed his wound. "You certainly do. Let me get the doctor." She hurried around from behind her desk, her footsteps echoing in the quiet old house, and knocked on the wooden door. Within a few moments, Doctor Phillips' gray head popped out of the door, his glasses falling down his nose as they so often did.

"Well, hello, Arlie. This is a pleasant surprise. Or, well, not so pleasant, it looks like," he said, staring at the stranger. "What happened?"

"He doesn't know," Arlie answered for him. "I found him out off of River Road. His head looks pretty bad. I thought it'd be better to bring him here rather than trying to make it to Arbordale."

The doctor stepped back, slipping gloves onto his hands from a box on the wall. "Come on in here," he said. "Let's get a look and see how deep it is." The man walked into the small room and Arlie took a seat outside of his office, watching as the door closed behind him.

"So, who was he?" Roberta asked. "I've never seen him around here."

"I...I don't know, actually," Arlie answered. "I think he's having a bit of memory loss from his wound. He doesn't seem to remember anything."

"How very strange," Roberta said, her mouse-like voice even higher than usual. "I'm sure the doctor will get him all fixed up. It was nice of you to stop, though I'm not sure it was the safest plan."

Arlie nodded. "Yeah, well, it's October third. Nothing's safe around here right now." She tried to smile, though she knew it came out stiff and she looked away. Roberta's voice grew quieter as she spoke again.

"How are you holding up, love? I know we're getting closer to..." She trailed off. It wasn't like she needed to say it. Each day that the anniversary drew nearer, Arlie could feel it in her bones. Another year had passed where she hadn't seen her husband's face, another year without his touch or hearing his voice. But, then again, she was hardly alone in her grief. Not in Crimson Falls, anyway. October thirteenth was a day where everyone was grieving. They'd all lost, and no one's grief was any larger than another's.

"One day at a time, right?" Arlie asked, because what else was there to say? "I'm just ready for this month to be over."

"Aren't we all?" Roberta said grimly. Just then, the door opened and Doctor Phillips walked out. He disappeared down a hallway, and Arlie looked into the room, where the stranger sat on the table.

"You okay in there?" she asked.

He smirked. "Getting there, I think."

"I'm going to get him bandaged," the doctor said, rounding the corner with a roll of gauze and tape in his hand. "But he's going to need to get staples." He smirked at the stranger. "You just got lucky enough with that placement that I can't help you. I can stop the bleeding as much as possible to hold you over until you get there." He walked back into the room, leaving the door open this time, and within a few moments, walked back out. This time, the man was behind him, gauze wrapped around his scalp to cover the wound.

"Do you guys have cabs around here?" he asked. "Or Uber?"

The doctor let out a chuckle, but stopped when he realized he was serious. "We can probably arrange for the police to get you there if you don't have a way."

Arlie stood up. "I can take him."

"No," the man said, touching the gauze. "You've done too much already. Honestly."

"I don't mind," she said. "You need to get checked out, and I'd hate to bother Chief Chapman with it when I'm perfectly capable. Besides, it'll be good research for me. For my next book."

Doctor Phillips nodded. "That's really kind of you, Arlie. And," he looked at the stranger, "it's probably the best possible plan. They'll want to see you as soon as possible to get in for a CT."

A FEW HOURS LATER, they were waiting for the emergency room doctor to return. The stranger had invited her to stay with him, and she'd gladly accepted. Anything for research. The doctors had to shave a bit of his hair in order to get the staples in place and clean him up. With the blood off of his face, she could finally take in the impossibly blue eyes. His black hair had been smoothed over and he sat up in his hospital bed, wearing just a gown and black socks. He was undeniably handsome in a regal way. Dignified. Clean cut. When she'd first seen him, it had been hard to gauge his age, though she assumed he couldn't be too young, but staring at him now, she realized he was closer to her age than she'd initially thought. As the dirt had been washed away, it took with it his seemingly gray hair and makeshift wrinkles. He couldn't have been more than forty-five.

"So," he said, clearing his throat, "you mentioned research for your books. What do you do?"

She smiled. She was never sure how to say it without sounding pompous, still feeling like a fraud despite her two years of success. "I'm an author."

"Seriously?" he asked, raising a brow and then wincing. "What do you write? Romance?"

She scowled. "Because I'm a woman?" It was a sensitive subject for her, especially after years of her publisher's insistence that she use a man's name to write. "I write thrillers."

He seemed impressed by that. "I knew you had a dark side."

"Do you read?"

He frowned, looking up as if trying to recall a memory. "I think so. God, this memory thing sucks."

"I'm wondering if you were mugged. I mean, not having a wallet on you, that's not normal."

"Your town doesn't exactly seem like the kind of place where people get mugged."

She crossed one leg over the other, letting out a breath. "Oh, you have no idea."

"Really now? Real life inspiration for your books, then?"

She laughed. "I guess you could say that. I feel like I should be asking you about yourself...but I guess there's no point."

"It would be the polite thing in normal circumstances, but rather impolite now, wouldn't it?" he asked with a grin. "I guess I could make up some heroic life story for myself, couldn't I?"

"I'd never know the difference."

"Alright, I'll play along. I was a...hm, a firefighter before. Named...Aaron?"

She stuck out her tongue.

"Not a fan?"

"If you're going to pick out your own name, surely you can come up with something better."

"How about Brock?"

"Too pretentious."

"Alright, Miss Author, make me a character. What would you name me?"

She thought for a moment, studying his features. "You're Mason. Mason Beaumont. A proper Southern gentleman with a large fortune. But you've broken away from it all in search of a simple life." She winked at him, crossing her arms.

"Mason Beaumont, huh?" he asked. "I like it. Now, tell me this…is Mason Beaumont a good guy or a bad guy?"

She gave him a small smile. "I guess we'll have to wait and see."

Just then, the door opened and the doctor walked in, a chart in his hand. "Okay, good news. It doesn't look like there's a bleed."

"Why don't you sound like that's a good thing?" Mason asked, reading Arlie's mind.

"Because it doesn't explain the memory loss." He paused. "It's probably nothing, but we do want to hold you for the night for observation. Hopefully we can get a better idea of what's going on and the best way to treat it."

"Does he need to stay awake? I could stay here and try to keep him—"

"No," the doctor answered, interrupting her. "That's an outdated course of action. We encourage them to sleep now; it lets the brain rest. But, not too much just yet. The police will be here soon to talk to you both."

Arlie nodded, adding that to her mental notes for her latest book. Could she work in a head injury somehow just to use that knowledge? Without another word, the doctor checked the monitors, typed something into his iPad, and walked out of the room. Arlie stood up. "Well, I guess I should be going then. I can wait out in the lobby to talk to the police if you want."

Mason nodded hesitantly. "You know, I don't mind if you stay. For…research or whatever."

Arlie just about jumped at the chance. "Are you sure?" She tried to look like it didn't mean as much to her as it did. She wasn't sure why she was so intrigued by this man, but she was. In the nearly two years since Brett had passed, her human interaction was extremely limited. She supposed it was part of the writer lifestyle, that people just assumed she was happy being alone, but it wasn't true. She craved conversation like an addiction. It had been too long since she'd had friends. Too long that she'd been inside her own head.

"Yeah. Sure. I mean, it's pretty lonely not knowing who you are. I think I'd like to be Mason for a while. And you're probably the only person who could understand that."

She smiled, sitting back down in her chair. "I can definitely understand that."

CHAPTER THREE

The next day, they were preparing to release Mason, though his memory still hadn't returned. Arlie walked into the room, handing over a clean shirt and pants she'd bought from a nearby store that Brett had loved.

Mason took them. "Thank you. I'll pay you back as soon as I figure out where all my money is."

She waved him off. "Honestly, it's not a big deal. They weren't much. Do you need me to drive you to a hotel?" He stared at her, and she realized her mistake as soon as she'd asked. "Right. No money. I could pay for it. You know, until you find your money or whatever."

"I can't ask you to do that," he said. "Arlie, you've done...more than I could ever expect from a total stranger. I'll figure something out."

"What are you going to figure out? You can't remember who you are. Even if you manage to find a job, you have nowhere to stay until you start getting paid. To leave you here alone with no ride anywhere and no clue who you are...it would be heartless. I can't do that. I'd never forgive myself."

"I'm not your responsibility," he said. "I really do appreciate it, but you've spent enough on me. Wasted enough time. I can't ask anymore from you."

"You aren't asking. I'm offering. If you won't let me pay for you to stay in a hotel, at least come and stay with me. I have plenty of room. That's probably safer anyway. People get a little crazy in Crimson Falls this time of year, and sometimes that crazy trickles over into Arbordale. Then, as soon as your memory comes back, I can help you get home."

"Why are you being so kind to me?" he asked, one brow raised.

"I can't say it's entirely selfless. It'll be nice to have some company. Not to sound like a *total* loser, but I'm always alone and this week is particularly hard for me. It's the anniversary of my husband's death. So, I could use the distraction."

"I'm so sorry," he said, his eyes softening. "I had no idea."

"It's okay."

He bit his lip. "Well, I'm happy to help distract you. At least I'll feel like I'm doing something useful, but please don't feel like you have to do this. I promise you I can take care of myself."

"Oh, I know," she said with a smile. "You were doing such a good job of that before I came along."

WHEN THEY ARRIVED at her house, Arlie led him into the

living room. It was a humble, brick home. Thirteen hundred square feet of improvements she had yet to make. Brett had promised he'd get around to it someday, and then when that someday was torn away from him, Arlie had never been able to hire it out. Despite the fact that money was no longer an issue, Arlie hadn't been able to leave the house they'd built. It was only six months ago that she'd finally packed up the last of Brett's clothes and put them into the attic. She couldn't even bring herself to get rid of them yet.

She set her purse and keys on the sofa table. "This is it. It's not much, but...it's home. The kitchen's there, bathroom's down the hall. I'm going to start something to eat. I'm starving. Any preferences? What do you like?"

"Your kindness is off-putting, Arlie. It's your house. You're hosting me. You could literally feed me stale chips and I would be grateful."

"What can I say? I'm a true Southern woman."

"Fix whatever you like. From what I can remember, I'm not picky."

She smiled. "My husband used to say that, too. Until I suggested something. Then he had four other suggestions," she said with a laugh. "So I guess I'm used to asking."

"Sometimes I think, as men, it's ingrained into us that we should know better than you. I'm sure he never meant to make you feel like you couldn't choose."

"No," Arlie agreed, "he didn't. My husband was a good man. An amazing man, actually. It was just a habit of his, you know? We all settle into our own habits."

"Can I ask what happened to him?"

Normally, Arlie hated to talk about it. The moment

she brought up his name, the people that recognized it—which was just about everyone—would get strange. Excited, but guilty for feeling excited. It was as if they knew him personally. As if it was them who sat with him at night eating ramen noodles on their worn couch. As if they were there when he'd hold her and they'd watch Jeopardy, competing to see who could answer the fastest. As if they loved him like she did. Didn't they know that was impossible?

But, as relief suddenly washed over her, she realized it couldn't hurt to tell Mason about Brett. Chances were, he wouldn't recognize the name even if he'd once known it. He was safe.

"He was…shot. At work. Some sort of domestic violence thing turned active shooter."

Mason's face grew stern, and he took a step toward her on what seemed like instinct. "I'm so sorry."

She took a step back, shaking her head. "It's okay."

"It's not okay."

"No, of course it's not okay," she said, acknowledging how easily the canned response slipped off her tongue.

"But people expect that you'll say that. If for no other reason than to make themselves feel better."

She nodded slowly. "'Fraid so."

"Well, I'm not like that. Or…at least, I don't think I am. You can be real with me. In fact, I want you to be. After all, at least while I've forgotten who I used to be, it's a chance for me to decide who I want to be moving forward. I'd like to think Mason is a good listener."

"Well, how does Mason, the good listener, feel about salmon?"

"Salmon sounds perfect," he said simply.

She nodded, her cheeks heating up at the way he was smiling at her, and suddenly she felt nervous. This would be the first time she'd had dinner with a man, alone, since Brett's death. It was the first time a man had ever stayed in her home that wasn't her husband. With nerves racing through her, she walked away quickly, trying hard to calm her pounding heart.

CHAPTER FOUR

T hat night at dinner, the couple ate ravenously. Arlie hadn't realized how hungry she was until the food was in front of her. She swirled her glass of wine. "I hope you like it. I'm not much of a cook." Judging by his already half-empty plate, he did.

"It's great," he said. "You shouldn't be so hard on yourself."

She took another bite. "So, I've been thinking about what your old life was like. Based on your clothes, I'm guessing maybe you were a lineman, or you worked construction? Do either of those seem right? The reflective vest...it has to mean something."

He pressed his lips together, apparently thinking while his fork remained in his hand. "Hm...maybe. It's like...it's all right there," he pointed to his temple, "but I just can't knock the clouds away enough to get a clear picture. Does that make sense?"

"None of this makes any sense, if I'm being honest. Two days ago I'd never met you. Today you're living in my house, and we know nothing about who you used to be. Do you have a family? People could be out there looking for you." She furrowed her brow, not sounding worried, but rather curious.

"Maybe. I watched the news the whole time we were in the hospital, though, and I never saw anything about me being missing. And you heard what the Arbordale police said, there are no missing persons reports that match my description. For all we know, I was just a bachelor who got hurt on the job."

"That doesn't make sense, though. Why wouldn't the people you work with report you missing? How would you have just wandered away from a worksite without anyone noticing you were hurt?"

"Those are all really great questions, Arlie. And I want to know the answers, too. I do. But, right now we don't know...and there's nothing we can learn tonight to help. So, I'd rather just enjoy each other's company. Enjoy this good food. The rest can wait for tomorrow."

She nodded. "Aren't you worried?"

"Are you?" He raised an eyebrow at her.

"I'm just fascinated by it, I guess. I mean...the idea that this can happen at any time to anyone. You could just walk away and forget your family and your life. It's terrifying."

"Unless there's nothing to forget," he mused quietly. She closed her eyes, feeling small tears forming. Sensing her distress, he leaned forward. "I'm so sorry, Arlie. I didn't mean to upset you. I wasn't thinking."

"No, I know you didn't. It's just...that's what my life has become, isn't it? If I disappeared...no one would miss me."

"That's not true."

"Of course it is," she insisted. "My husband's dead. I have no children, no real friends. My only living relative is my mother, and she's in a nursing home with dementia. She doesn't know who I am most days, let alone whether I'm missing. I don't have coworkers. Aside from checking in with my agent once a month, if I were to go missing, there's no one that would even notice."

"Even if that was true, it's not any more. I'm going to notice now. Do you honestly think you could get rid of me that easily? You saved my life. You've been kinder to me than anyone I can remember. You've brought me to your home, bought me new clothes, fed me...I'm your friend, Arlie. And that means it's my job to notice when you disappear."

She laughed, so caught up in the tension she almost hadn't noticed his smirk. "Thanks."

He sat back, looking more relaxed. "Besides, I'm not so sure a reclusive life is a bad thing. From what I can tell, people are generally assholes."

"Yeah," she agreed, "that's true. They are."

"But not you."

She took another bite. "Not me. And hopefully not you."

"The old me, maybe. But definitely not Mason Beaumont."

"I like Mason," she said with a wink. "Mason would make an excellent character."

"Well, I should think you would. You created him." With that, he took another drink of his wine. Her belly quickly filled with warmth as she stared at him. Did he realize she might've been flirting? *Was she?*

23

CHAPTER FIVE

A few days later, Arlie lay in bed, her computer on her lap. She desperately needed to get a couple thousand words down, especially with the setback she'd had the past couple of days. It wasn't entirely Mason's fault, though that had certainly made it challenging. This week was always hard for her. It was as if the words just stopped flowing for a while. But they'd be back. Once the week was over, and even better once the month was over, her story would flow again. Not that anything seemed to flow like it had when Brett was alive, but it was enough.

She sat up, listening to his footsteps down the hall. It felt strange, having someone else in the house again. Strange, yet oddly comforting—knowing someone else was there. Knowing this Founders Day wouldn't be spent alone. Knowing she was safe—er, safer, at least. Knowing she had someone to protect her.

From what?

What would she need protecting from? It had been the same last year, but she'd foolishly thought this Founders

Day would be different. Since Brett had died, the fear that had always been there this time of year was amplified by a thousand. She didn't like to think of how she'd spent the entire month of October last year—hiding out in her room, crying for days on end. It was like she had lost her husband all over again. For her, October thirteenth spent alone was harder than Christmas spent alone. At the end of the month, she'd dropped thirty pounds from her already small frame. That's what not eating got you, she supposed. But when you're fearing for your life, your entire resolve being torn from you every morning as you wake up and realize the man you love, the man you need, isn't there—will never be there again—food is the last thing on your mind. She closed her eyes again, shaking the thought from her brain. She was being paranoid. That's what this time of year did to her. It made her worry. It made her watch over her shoulder. It made her come to terms with her own mortality. How she was just one day, one second, away from everything ending. Like that.

The morning Brett had died, she'd planned out their dinner for that evening. She'd known what they were going to do the weekend after. They'd put down a deposit on their cruise the next summer. Their life was planned... and just like that, it wasn't. It was over. Everything. Everything she had pictured for their future ended, and there was nothing she would ever be able to plan with the man she loved ever again.

But that wasn't going to happen to her. She was safe. She was indoors. She had someone here who could protect her from all the bad outside. If it were up to her, though she'd never admit it to him, she and Mason would stay indoors until the first of November. Until they were safe again.

She climbed from bed, stepping out into the hall and quickly shutting the door behind her. What was he doing up so late? She walked up the small set of stairs that led from her bedroom to the hallway and looked around. The light to her office was on, and she turned the handle, sticking her head in.

Brett had helped her set up the office, once just a small room with a worn, brown recliner and a pressed wood desk they'd bought in a box. Her work chair had been so uncomfortable she'd had to switch from it and the desktop to the recliner and her ancient laptop and back again just to get comfortable. Now, the room was supposed to be her sanctuary. At least, it was set up like one. A white, faux fur rug lay in the center of the room, a large wooden desk on the far side. Her luxury leather writing chair sat behind it, gold trim lining both the chair and the desk. In the other corner, an oversized white recliner and gorgeous end table sat, and further down was a gray and white couch. It was the largest bedroom in the house, and Arlie had made great use of the space. Overall, it was a writer's dream, and exactly what Arlie thought she needed to get back in the groove of things. After all, what else did she need to spend the money on? Brett's life insurance had paid off most of their debt, and her measly existence didn't accumulate the large bills she'd once pictured rolling in from a lavish lifestyle. But, the office hadn't worked. In fact, most of her words were written in her bed, the bed that had been shared with Brett. Many times she'd wondered if he had been her muse. If the words would only flow around him and, with him gone, she was doomed to never pump out another story.

But now, another man sat in her office. Mason, wearing Brett's plaid pajama pants and a white t-shirt, spun around in her chair, nearly jumping at the sight of her.

"Oh, I'm sorry," he said, dropping the paperback in his hands. It was a copy of her debut novel, *Say Goodbye.* "Did I wake you?"

"No," she said, crossing her arms and staring him down. "What are you doing in here?"

"I didn't mean to...intrude. I...I wanted to read one of your books. See what makes the famous Arlie Montgomery so famous." He smiled nervously, standing from the chair. "I should've asked first. I'm really sorry, Arlie. It was rude of me to just assume I could come into your space."

"It's fine," she said, though she wasn't entirely sure that was true. "It's not really my space, anyway. It should've been," she said, "but when the entire house is silent, you don't really need a place to escape to."

He swallowed, picking up the book from the desk and closing it. He tapped the cover with his forefinger. "This is...it's really good. You're an excellent writer."

"Do you read thrillers?" she asked, though she slapped a hand to her forehead quickly. "Sorry."

"It's okay," he said with a nervous laugh. "I don't know if I used to, but I'm certainly interested in them now."

She sank into the couch, waving a hand to get him to sit, too. "What part are you at?"

He opened the book back up, flipping through a few pages until he found his place. "Here. Roarke has just

27

found the body. Corkscrew to the neck, huh? That's a nice touch."

She laughed. "What can I say? I'm a sucker for a good murder scene."

"I can tell. And this detective...is she supposed to be you?"

"Me? Of course not."

"She reminds me of you," he said simply. "The way I picture her."

"And how is that?" she asked, leaning forward and hanging on his every word. Discussing her books never got old.

"She's...brunette,   of   course,   like   you. Smart...distrusting..."

"You think I'm distrusting?"

"Aren't you?" he asked.

"I don't think so. I mean, you're here, aren't you?"

"Yeah," he said, "but I don't know if that's because you trust me or because you're trying to use me for research."

She cocked her head to the side slowly, not entirely sure either. "Does anyone really trust anyone these days?"

"Good point. Maybe trusting the wrong person is what got me here." He pointed to his head.

"Maybe. Trouble is deciding who's deserving of your trust and who's going to screw you over."

"I'm not going to screw you over, Arlie," he said, his voice low. He wheeled the chair around from behind the desk, leaning closer to her.

"I hope not."

"I could never," he said. "I'm...I want to be everything you want. I want to be Mason for you. I think you deserve a Mason." His blue eyes burned into hers, causing her to look away suddenly. "I'm sorry," he said softly. "Was that too much?"

She shook her head. "No, it's just...sometimes it's easy to forget this isn't real."

He placed his hand on her cheek, turning her face to look at him. "Who says it's not real?"

She stared at him, their faces only inches apart. He wasn't moving his hand, and it was causing her dangerous thoughts to surface. "Eventually," she said, speaking slowly, "you're going to remember who you were. And then you're going to leave me to go back to your old life."

"What if I don't want that to happen? What if my old life was nothing special?"

"Life with me wouldn't be anything special."

Without warning, his lips were on hers, his hands cupping her face. It took her a moment to process what was happening, her body frozen in place. His fingers laced through her hair, pulling her further into his kiss, and she seemed to wake up. She thawed quickly, placing her hands on his neck. His kiss was unfamiliar, though that was a surprisingly good thing. The stubble around his chin rubbed her lips, and his mouth fit perfectly on hers. It shocked her how easily she could give in to him, but perhaps it was more about giving in to herself. Giving in to what she'd wanted for so long.

It had been years since anyone had touched her the way he was touching her now. Years since she felt another person's warmth. Though she wished, desperately, that it could've been Brett holding her this way, she was surprised to find that she wasn't thinking of him in that moment. All that seemed to matter was Mason. Mason's hands. Mason's lips. Mason's tongue. Mason.

Just as she began to lose herself in the intoxicating kiss, he stopped, pulling his lips from hers. His heavy breath still hit her mouth, his lips red and mere inches from hers. "I'm sorry. I shouldn't have done that."

"What? Why?" she asked, her eyes flickering up to meet his.

"Because...you've been so kind to me. I should not have assumed that means you want to...to do whatever this is. I don't want things to get awkward, or to make you feel like I'm overstepping."

"Mason, stop. You aren't overstepping. And if I didn't want to kiss you, I wouldn't have."

"Oh, really?" he asked, his gaze moving to her mouth at her words.

"Really," she promised as his lips met hers again. With that, he set the book down, sliding on top of her so she laid down on the couch. Her back pressed into the stiff, unfamiliar leather, sending shivers down her spine.

He ran a hand over the side of her face, kissing her playfully. "Well, then, let me thank you properly."

She rubbed her nose against his. "Do your damnedest."

CHAPTER SIX

The next morning, Arlie's eyes fluttered open slowly, and she stared around the room. It took a minute for her to register that she was naked, and in doing so, her cheeks flushed, and she pulled the blanket up to cover her chest.

She lifted her head from the pillow, staring at the empty place next to her. For the first time in two years, the name that popped into her head first was not Brett's.

Mason.

She sat up further, keeping the blanket over her chest and staring at the messy bed, the indentation where his body had been. He'd been there, right? She hadn't dreamed last night up? Dreamed him up entirely, maybe. Judging by the soreness of her unused body, she was pretty sure that wasn't the case.

Had she really waited two years to have sex again? God, she hadn't realized how much she needed it. How much she needed last night.

Then it hit her. Last night. Sex. Sex with a stranger.

Sex with a stranger she'd just met. Sex with a stranger she'd just met in a bed she'd bought with Brett. Brett who she loved. Brett whose ring she still wore on the chain around her neck.

She closed her eyes, resting her face in her palm and sucking in a breath. What on earth was she thinking? She laid back in bed, pondering her thoughts, trying to decide how she felt. Or maybe, how she should feel.

How much could she really trust this man, anyway? More than anyone, he could hurt her. She'd let him in, in a way she'd refused to let anyone in for so long. She'd given him access to her life and her body. She'd made herself vulnerable.

She let out a sigh, standing up from the bed and pulling her shorts and robe on over herself. Try as she might, she couldn't find it in herself to regret what had happened. It had been good after all. Really, really good.

Mason was...dreamy. And patient. Attentive. He took care of her in a way Brett had slacked off on.

Oh. She squeezed her eyes shut, shaking her head. Enough with the comparisons. Brett was her husband. Mason was still a stranger.

Last night didn't change that. No matter how good he tasted. Or how amazing his tongue felt against her...

Stop. Memories of the night flooded her mind no matter how hard she tried to push them away, and she realized her fatal mistake. She was falling for him.

Hard.

Fast.

Damn, she was like a teenage boy, bringing every thought back to sex. Good sex. Life-changing sex.

Get it together, woman.

She padded down the hallway, wondering where on earth he might be, and stopped when she saw the light on under her office door once again. It was like déjà vu.

Hey, if they could relive the night again, she certainly wasn't going to complain—

For the love of God, woman. Do you need a cold shower or what?

She grinned, feeling practically giddy with her horny little self. Whatever Mason had done to her, it was the most alive she'd felt in so long.

She pressed the door open quickly. "Good morning," she said with a smile, seeing his face. He was behind her desk again. He looked up at her, slamming the laptop closed quickly.

"What's up?" she asked, walking around to him.

He shook his head, pulling her down into a kiss and helping her slide onto his lap. "Sorry, that's the universal sign for watching porn, isn't it?"

She kissed him back. "A little bit, yeah."

"I was…just trying to do some research into missing people. You know, who I might be, or whatever."

"In a hurry to get back to your old life?" she asked, feeling uneasy. Why was his face so red?

"Not at all," he said, resting his forehead on hers. "The exact opposite, actually."

"Meaning what?" She cocked her head to the side.

"Meaning…I'm hoping they don't ever find my old life. Or, that there's no life out there for them to find. I don't ever want to leave you, Arlie. Last night…last night was—"

"Amazing," she finished for him.

"Yeah," he said, the corners of his mouth turning up

into a grin as he slid his hand out to cup her cheek. "Yeah, it really was. And...I guess I keep waiting for the other shoe to drop and this to all be over."

She swallowed, not wanting to admit how much the thought terrified her. "I guess we just have to make the most of the time we have together, then."

"I don't know how much time could ever be enough," he whispered, his lips practically brushing hers.

"No amount of time is ever enough when you know you have to say goodbye."

"I don't know if I ever can."

She closed her eyes. "Me either." She'd said goodbye once before, and it had damn near killed her.

CHAPTER SEVEN

L ater that day, Arlie took Mason to town, despite her complete aversion to doing so this time of year. He insisted on seeing more of the town, hoping to jog a memory or two, and though she'd warned him about the craziness that surrounded downtown at this time of the month, he was certain this was what he wanted.

As they walked through the quiet town square, the hair on Arlie's arms stood on end. Something was going to happen. Something bad. She just knew it. They were the only two people crazy enough to be out right now. Granted, it was just past ten a.m. on a Tuesday, but still.

He took her hand, leading her to the gazebo that sat in the middle of town. At one time not so long ago, it had been kept up, but now it was in desperate need of a paint job and new boards in a few places. She stepped over one particularly loose-looking board and took a seat next to him. "Are you happy now?" she asked. "You've seen the big city of Crimson Falls."

He wrapped an arm around her shoulders, looking off into the distance. "I think it's cute."

She snorted. Sometimes it was, she supposed. In February when they had their annual Be My Valentine Festival, the townspeople decorated the entire square with heart-shaped balloons and red and pink decor. It was cute then. Christmastime was usually well thought out and adorable. They even hired a Santa to visit with the children. But, October Crimson Falls was not 'cute.' Desolate. Gray. Gloomy. Terrifying. Those were words she would use to describe it. But not 'cute.' Never 'cute.'

"You're a bad liar," she said simply. "Any of this bringing back any memories?"

He shook his head. "Nope. You were right."

"I told you I know everyone in Crimson Falls," she said smugly, running her fingers through the side of his hair.

"You weren't kidding. I can't get over how quiet it is out here," he said simply. "You were right about that too."

"October isn't safe."

"Well, let's get you home where it is safe," he said, and she sighed loudly with relief. "Do you mind if we stop in here for a minute, though?" He pointed to the Crooked Crow, a small bar in town owned by the biggest ass Arlie had ever met.

"Oh, no, not there," she said, and then realized she probably sounded a bit like a drama queen. "I mean... Perry's not the most friendly guy you'll ever meet."

"Perry?"

"The bar owner. Big guy. Tattoos. Total jerk."

He snickered.

"What?"

"Did you really say 'jerk'? You're so cute."

She smacked his arm playfully. "Hush."

"It's so funny. Your books are this dark, twisted, terrifying part of you...but on the outside, you're so...*sunshine-y.*"

"*Sunshine-y?*" She looked down, biting her lip. "Everyone has two sides."

Without her realizing it, they were nearing the bar, and Mason stopped at the door. "I'm going to run in here real quick. You can wait outside if you want."

"*No,*" she said, probably too quickly. "I'll go with you."

"I'll take care of you, Arlie," he said, his voice sincere as he pulled open the door.

The small, dark room smelled of vomit and floor cleaner and, if Arlie had wanted to, she could've bet her month's royalties that the men in the bar were the ones she could've predicted would be there. The alcoholics who never left, the husbands avoiding their wives, and the old men who just needed somewhere to be around other people.

"Well, if it isn't our little celebrity." Perry sneered from behind the bar, picking something from his teeth as he spoke. "Who's this?"

"Mason," Mason answered quickly, approaching the bar and holding out a hand. Perry stared at him without offering to shake it. "I, um, I'm new in town. A friend of Arlie's."

"So?" Perry barked. "You here to drink, or what?"

Mason looked at the clock on the wall, not bothering to mention that it was only ten a.m., but Arlie knew he was thinking it. "Nope. Just wanted to see if you were hiring. I could use a bit of work."

Arlie winced, wishing she'd known why he was

coming there. She could've warned him that Perry wouldn't hire him. He rarely hired. She was pretty convinced he lived in the bar.

To her surprise, Perry cocked his head to the side. "You a bartender?"

"I can open a beer as easily as the next guy," he said, glancing around, "and from the looks of this place, no one is ordering anything too complicated."

Arlie was sure he was going to punch him. Perry didn't have a sense of humor, he never had, but he shocked her again by letting out a loud laugh.

"Okay, sure, kid." He called him 'kid,' though Arlie was still convinced Mason must've been close to forty. "You can work here. Can you start tonight?"

"You got it," Mason said, reaching out to shake his hand again. This time, Perry took it, shaking his hand slowly.

"Be here by six," he instructed. With that, Mason turned, walking from the building with Arlie's fingers laced between his.

"Why would you want to work there? It's not exactly safe."

"I need money," he said with a shrug. "I can't keep letting you pay for everything. And from what I know, bars are usually a place where you can make easy money without having to answer too many questions. As in, the whole 'not having an ID or social security number' thing shouldn't matter to...what did you say his name was?"

"Perry."

"Right. Perry. He didn't seem too concerned with my background, and since I can't seem to remember mine, it's probably a perfect fit."

CHAPTER EIGHT

That night, Arlie watched Mason walk out the door, his hands in the pockets of Brett's old jeans. She felt nostalgic, remembering the many times she'd watched Brett walk out the door on his way to work. Was this a betrayal to him? It couldn't be, could it? She was allowed to move on. Expected to move on. What choice did she have? She was still young, just shy of thirty-seven, and she'd put her husband in the ground almost two years ago. She couldn't be expected to mourn him forever. Then again, she was pretty sure she would. Though the daily rounds of crying had stopped, and she was functioning more and more like a human, Arlie was not over her husband. She was still very much in love with the man who had loved her first. The man who had loved her best.

But Mason was a nice distraction, as crass as that sounded. He was kind and funny and so easy to talk to. It didn't hurt that he was also extremely easy to look at. It *also* didn't hurt that he was a...what was the phrase she'd used in her novels? *A master in the sheets.* God, just thinking about the way he touched her gave her cold chills. It was unreal how good he was. Or maybe it had just been so long for her that anyone would seem impossibly good.

She sank into the couch, pulling her laptop to her lap and opening it. She'd already decided to scrap the story she'd been working on, finding a new story in her latest muse. She typed the first words, losing herself in her words for the first time in so long. Maybe it was true, that her best work had come from being inspired by Brett, because now the story was flowing from being in Mason's presence like it hadn't in so long. Was she entirely useless on her own?

After a few hours of writing, and nearly five thousand words written—*holy cow!*—Arlie closed the laptop, covering her eyes to allow them to adjust to the lack of light.

Her phone was going off, its vibrations echoing through the quiet house, and she stood, walking to the kitchen countertop where it lay and picked it up. "Hello?"

"Arlie, darling, sorry it's taken so long to get in touch. How's the book coming?" It was her agent, Phoebe. The one who was supposed to call two weeks ago. The one Arlie was glad hadn't called, as she had absolutely nothing new to report.

"Hey, Phoebe, no problem. I've actually just started a new project. I had to step away from the first one—it just wasn't coming to me—but this one's flowing nicely. I'm at around twenty thousand words," she bit her lip at the lie, promising to get there soon, "but it's nothing like I've ever written before. I really think it's going to be a hit."

"That's fabulous, honey." Phoebe always called her little terms of endearment, like 'honey,' 'darling,' and 'sweetheart,' even though she was nearly the exact same age as Arlie. "Look, I want to be supportive, and you know I'll love whatever you put out, but you do have to put out something. And soon. Sales are dropping pretty rapidly. That's the business, you know? You had a great year and then a decent year, but these last few months… well, things are headed south. We need to put something new out quickly. What kind of a timeline are you thinking?"

"Nine months?" Arlie asked, knowing she was pushing it. When Phoebe didn't respond right away, Arlie corrected herself. "Maybe six."

"Okay," Phoebe said hesitantly. "I'm sure it will be fine. Let's check back in next week and see where you are, okay? Write, write, write. Love you, doll face." With that, the line was dead and Arlie was left in silence again.

Phoebe was right. She knew, her sales were pitiful lately, almost back to what they'd been before her career took off. The money she'd made from her success was great, and it would last her for quite a while, but it would eventually run out. Especially if she didn't put something new out. If she wasn't able to do it soon, she was pretty convinced Phoebe would give up on her. Their contract would be running out soon. And what could she expect, really? She hadn't put out anything new in over a year, and she couldn't even make it to the halfway point in anything she was currently working on. Every time, as she grew nearer to forty thousand words, her brain shut down. Suddenly, every word she typed was mush. Pitiful. Unworthy of other eyes.

She groaned. Honestly, what was the point? Maybe she'd be better off getting a day job. She could survive off a few meaningless hours at the local grocery store, or maybe she could venture to Arbordale and find an office job. It wouldn't be so hard. In fact, it would be a hell of a lot easier than doing what she did. Dreaming, mostly. Dreaming and writing and scrapping what she'd written, and sending it to her editor and agent and getting it torn apart by them, and getting bad reviews and no one understanding what she was trying to say. No one understanding that she was begging for help because she was so incredibly alone, and her husband, the only man who had cared to understand, was dead and she was by herself for the first time since she was eighteen. Her entire life had been spent on her books, not on her marriage, and oh, she had so much resentment for that and all she'd missed and given up just to get a few more words in. All this for what? To accomplish a dream she'd had once? Did she even care about the dream anymore? She'd gotten it. Her books had earned her more money than she could've ever hoped for, people knew her name, and yet…it felt empty. Everything she'd dreamed of had been handed to her in a box with a little bow, but it had come at the cost of her husband, the life she'd pictured with him. With that knowledge, she wasn't sure she could ever feel the love for writing she once had.

But at the end of the day, she was terrified to go out of her house too much, and Arbordale was the town where Brett had taken his last breath, so it felt too emotional to make it a part of her daily routine. She was trapped in the life she'd wished for, the life she hadn't realized she could hate so much.

She walked to her computer, picking it up again and wanting to get lost in the only thing that could make her feel better. *Where were we, Mason Beaumont?*

CHAPTER NINE

She opened her eyes, feeling the laptop lift off her lap, her vision blurry from sleeping in her contacts. She stared at him, confused for a second, and then awake. "Hey," she said, rubbing her eyes and sitting up further on the couch. The morning light was creeping in from behind the blinds.

"Hey." Mason kissed her forehead, closing the laptop. "Sleep good?"

"I did," she said, and it wasn't entirely a lie this time. "How was work?"

"I could call Perry several names worse than 'jerk,'" he told her, "but it wasn't bad." He reached in his pocket, pulling out several twenties and offering them to her. "Here. Take it. It's not all that I owe you, but it's some."

"Mason, honestly, I don't need that. You don't owe me anything." Her eyes lit up. "Actually, *you've* given *me* something." She pulled the laptop to her again, lifting the lid and checking her word count. "I'm at fifteen thousand words. In one night. I don't know if that's ever happened to me before."

"Thanks to me?"

"Yes," she said, feeling her face flush with color. "You inspire me."

"Well, I'm happy to help," he said with a wink. "Speaking of, I finished book two. Two down, two to go."

"You already finished?" She swallowed, nerves rushing through her. It never went away, that overwhelming sense of excitement and fear that filled her at hearing someone had read her books.

"In between customers last night. Perry wasn't entirely happy, but he didn't say anything. What can I say? You're really talented, Arlie. I can't put them down."

"You have no idea what it means to me, the fact that you even read them. So many people in my life, even now, six years after I started publishing, they still tell me they're going to read my books *someday*. I think it's almost worse for them to say that than for them to just say nothing at all."

He slid onto the couch beside her, kissing her lips carefully, his hand on her jaw. "Well, they don't know what they're missing. And I can't wait to see what you'll come up with next."

She sighed, remembering her conversation with Phoebe last night.

"What's wrong?" he asked, sensing the shift in her mood.

"Nothing," she said softly, but his eyes narrowed at her and made her want to share her burden with him. "It's just...since Brett died, I've really had trouble writing. Last night was amazing progress, but I'm still not where I need to be, you know? And it's not like my books are getting any more popular. And I'm not putting anything new out. And my agent's getting frustrated and my publisher's starting to give up on me and it just feels like I don't know what I want to do anymore. Or who I want to be. As a writer. Or a person." She placed her face into her palms, groaning. "I'm sorry. I'm not making any sense."

"No," he said, "you are. You're making total sense."

"I am?"

"You are." His thumb was caressing her cheek, and she closed her eyes, losing herself in the sensation. "Of course," he said, "I'm not sure I'm the most reliable judge, you know, being that my mind is an empty slate and all."

"Oh, yeah," she said with a laugh. "Well, I trust your judgement anyway." She paused. "What are we going to do about that? About you. Aren't you worried? I would be a nervous wreck if I were you."

"What's there to be nervous about?" he asked with a shrug. "I mean, of course I want to know who I am, or who I was, but I'm okay. This…what we have…it's good. If anything, like I told you before, I'm nervous about having to give this all up for my old life. How could anyone be as good as you?"

She looked down, the butterflies in her stomach more active than ever. "I just feel like there's more we should be doing."

"Like what?" he asked. "We don't even know where to start looking. The police know about me. They're trying to track down any employers who've worked in that part of town lately, someone who might be missing me. They're checking missing persons reports. They've run my fingerprints and DNA, and we should hopefully be hearing back, but they said there's little else that can be done. Even on their end. So, what else is there for us to do but wait?"

She shook her head, knowing he was right. "I guess that's true. I just feel so useless."

"You aren't useless, Arlie. You've helped me so much. Given me a place to stay. You're helping me get a new start until we find out where I belong."

"So, we just wait, then? You're okay with that?"

"I'm perfectly okay with it," he assured her. "But no one said we can't have a little fun while we wait." His hand slid up her shirt, his lips grazing her skin, and she let her worries go for the moment. Nothing mattered besides Mason. Mason and her. Her and Mason.

And her books. And his past.

No.

Mason.

Mason.

Mason.

CHAPTER TEN

"Why don't we get out of Crimson Falls for the rest of the weekend?" Mason asked, staring at her over the kitchen table.

"What?" She took a bite of her bacon, staring back.

"We could get away. Go on vacation or whatever. Head to the beach. Head to the mountains. Head somewhere."

She bit her lip, thinking about how amazing it might be to get away from Crimson Falls during this week. Arlie had never been the kind of person who wanted to leave the town totally. She felt at home here. It was the only place she'd ever felt accepted, but since Brett's passing, the town brought more grief than happiness. Could she leave? Could she get away? Escape with Mason and never look back? Would a vacation be enough if she were to truly leave? She wasn't sure. Leaving Crimson Falls would be like breathing fresh air, and she wasn't sure she'd want to come back to the pollution once she'd escaped it. "I don't know."

"Come on," he coaxed. "What's your favorite vacation spot?"

She shook her head. "I don't know. Honestly, I've never really been on vacation."

"What do you mean? Never?"

"Well, growing up with a single mother who worked two and three jobs just to scrape by, we never really had a lot of money to spend on vacations, and then Brett and I struggled, too. He always wanted to support my dream, he wanted me home writing, so he took a corporate IT job, even though teaching was always his passion. And…even though it paid pretty well, we were in tremendous debt from both of our degrees and small loans here and there, plus our cars, so it just…we were barely above water." She blushed. "I'm sorry, I don't know why I'm telling you all of this. A simple 'no' would've been fine, huh?"

"I never mind learning more about you, Arlie. I find you fascinating."

"Fascinating, hmm?" she asked with a wink. "No one's ever used *that* word to describe me."

"Well, I just did," he said. "And I finished your last book, by the way. I think it was my favorite yet."

"Really?" She beamed. "Mine too, actually. Brett liked the second one best, but I always connected with the last."

He suddenly sported a devilish grin. "Well, I think that says a lot about you."

"Why's that?" she asked. "Because it's about a writer?"

"No, because there are some…pretty racy scenes." He looked away, as if he were embarrassed, but when he looked back, his eyes were full of fire. "It's pretty hard to believe all of *that* came out of this." He tapped her forehead.

"You don't think I can be...*racy?*" she asked, rubbing a bit of bacon grease across her bottom lip slowly. It was meant to be a joke, but the tension between them was suddenly very real.

He leaned in, grasping her head and forcing his lips to hers. The heat grew rapidly as he lifted her to the table, shoving the food out of the way. She heard a plate crash to the ground but didn't bother to look at the mess. In that moment, nothing mattered. She wrapped her legs around his back, tangled her fingers in his hair, and let out a groan. His strong arms were around her, his lips trailing down her neck.

"You know..." he whispered, his voice vibrating against her skin, "thank God for those sex scenes. Now I know *exactly* what you like."

She closed her eyes as one of his hands slid down her thigh, her insides on fire for him. She let out a sigh as his lips left hers, and he lifted her shirt, his kisses trailing down her belly. She sat up, wanting to feel his lips on hers again, and he stopped, staring at her and pushing her back down, his icy blue eyes growing dark with passion. He was right, this was like a scene from one of her books. What could she say? She liked men who expected to be in control. "Don't move a muscle," he told her, "or I'll stop." His lips were on hers again, his hand sliding under the elastic band of her pajama pants.

A knock on the door interrupted them, their lips parting with breathless gasps. "Expecting someone?" Mason asked, looking as disappointed as Arlie felt. She sat up from the table, wiping her mouth and shaking her head.

"Not that I know of." She hopped down to the floor,

tiptoeing across the carpet and peering through the navy curtains. She turned around suddenly, staring at him with a furrowed brow. "It's...it's the police. Do you think they've found out who you are?"

Without waiting for an answer, she swung the door open, staring into Chief Chapman's tired, dark eyes. "Chief Chapman, good morning." She put her arms around herself, feeling self-conscious.

"Good morning, Arlie," he said, scratching his head. "I'm sorry to wake you. Do you have a minute?"

"Oh, of course," she said, not bothering to explain that her messy hair was not from sleep. Instead, she took a step back, allowing him to pass by her. "Is everything all right?"

"I'm afraid not," he said, his lips pressed together as he turned around to face her. "Founders Day is in full force."

Her skin went cold, suddenly knowing what he was going to say. "Something's happened?" It wasn't about Mason at all. Had her car been vandalized? Had her house? She hadn't heard anyone outside. Then again, she hadn't been paying too much attention.

"I'm afraid so," he said, and there was that word again. *Afraid.* Like a warning. "Perry was murdered last night."

"*What?*" she and Mason asked at the same time.

The chief looked between them both. "We found him this morning."

"Oh, no," Arlie gasped, touching her chest. Was she supposed to feel bad? Sure, it was terrible, but no one in town cared about Perry. Not the wife he'd abused for years, not the girls at the bar that he mistreated constantly, not the townspeople who he verbally attacked daily. He was a bad guy. And, try as she might, Arlie couldn't summon up one kind thought about him.

Luckily, Mason spoke up, interrupting the silence. "What happened?"

"He was shot. Behind his bar. It happened sometime last night, and I know a few of the guys mentioned that you've been working there...did you see anything?"

"I didn't," Mason answered. "I didn't work last night. I wasn't scheduled to go back in until tonight. Is the bar closed? I can run over and keep things going until..." He trailed off, and Arlie wasn't sure where he was planning to go with that. Until what? Perry wasn't coming back to run the place. Whose responsibility would it be now? Would the bar close? She shuddered at the mere idea of it. Crimson Falls without a bar was like Christmas without a tree.

The chief nodded. "No, we've got it closed down for a while. Open investigation and all. I'm not sure when you'll be able to go back. We'll have to see what the wife wants to do. Anyway, you confirmed what Herman and Ronnie said. About you not being there. They were there all night and never saw you. But I wanted to be sure." He sighed. "We all know this is how this time of year goes. People just lose their minds." He pressed his fingers into the bridge of his wrinkled nose. "And we know Perry isn't exactly the most liked man in town, so we have no shortage of suspects, but I wondered if you'd seen anything that seemed odd to you? Any fights with customers? Any altercations that may have caused you suspicion? Most of the men in that bar are either too drunk or scared to tell the truth, so we wanted to ask you."

Mason thought for a moment before shaking his head. "I can't think of anything. I mean, the guy's an ass. But, he seems—seemed—to get along well enough with the patrons."

"Okay, well, if you think of anything, just give me a call. Arlie has my number."

"Yeah, of course."

The chief nodded. "Well, you all take care, okay? Let me know if you hear anything."

"You've got it," Arlie promised, opening the door with shaking hands. When the chief was out of earshot, she looked to Mason. "Thank God you weren't there last night. It could've been you."

"I know," Mason said. "I can't believe no one saw anything. That bar is far from empty every night."

Arlie shrugged. "No one saw anything, or no one wants to say what they saw. People in Crimson, even though we're small, don't typically like to stick our necks out for other people. Not when those same people could hurt us later."

"But who would want to hurt Perry?"

"Better question: who wouldn't?" she asked, frowning at the grim joke. "I know that's harsh...but honestly, I'm surprised it didn't happen sooner. The guy is a jerk." She looked up at him, a thought hitting her. "I don't want you going back there."

"What do you mean? It's my job. If I don't go back, who will keep it going? It's not like I have many options for employment in Crimson Falls."

"It's not your responsibility. I told you this town is dangerous right now. You need to stay here. Where you're safe."

He wrapped her into a hug. "I'm sorry. I know how hard this must be on you. All the memories it has to be bringing up."

"You have no idea," she said, small tears forming in her eyes suddenly. They weren't for Perry. They'd never be for Perry. No. These tears were, as always, for herself and all that she'd lost.

CHAPTER ELEVEN

The next day, on October twelfth, the second murder happened. This time, when the chief knocked on her door, he was accompanied by another officer. Someone young. A boy Arlie hardly recognized.

"Arlie." The chief greeted her as she swung open the door, this time dressed slightly better than before and with her hair freshly combed.

"Someone else?" she asked, looking behind her to where Mason stood.

"I'm afraid so," he said softly. "Darla Redding, a second grade teacher at the school."

"Oh no," Arlie said, and this time her shock felt more real. She knew Darla. Not well, but well enough. Enough to care. "Oh no."

The chief placed a hand on her shoulder. "We need to talk to you."

"What about?" she asked. She had nothing to do with Darla, and neither did Mason. She couldn't imagine what this visit could be pertaining to...but by the look on his face, she knew it couldn't be good.

"You'll want to sit for this," he told her, pointing to the chair with his free hand. She followed his instructions, sitting in the worn recliner. Mason took her hand, looking back and forth between her and the chief. "Now, this is going to sound crazy. Crazier than usual, anyway." He pressed his lips together, his mustache buzzing with a deep exhale. "You'll forgive me for saying this, but I've never read your books. I'm not much of a reader. I can read fine, but never comprehend what I read," he said. It was the same old excuse she heard time and time again, and so she nodded, waiting for the lies to end. "But my wife, you know Anita loves them. And...well, she pointed something out after this case. Something that can't be ignored."

"Something? Something like what?" Her palms were sweating at his tone and she rubbed them over her jeans carefully.

"When Perry was killed, he was shot in the back behind the bar. Not that suspicious, I guess. But then Darla died. And the murder weapon was a corkscrew to the neck." He stared at her, waiting for her to catch on. It didn't take long and she was gasping.

"What? No." She shook her head, her fingertips dancing over her lips.

"Yes," the chief confirmed. "It's crazy, I know, but both murders are eerily similar to the ones in your books." He pressed his lips together under the large mustache. "And I'm afraid that's something we can't ignore anymore."

"What are you saying?" she asked softly.

"I think we have a copycat on our hands, Arlie.

Someone who is using your books as inspiration to commit crimes. Murders."

"But...why would someone do that?" she asked. "And why now? Do you think it's because of Founders Day? So many years after the books were published? That doesn't make any sense, but it's too big a coincidence, right?"

"We don't know," he said. "Right now it's all just speculation, but we'd like to have you come down to the station so we can discuss this further." He looked up to where Mason stood. "And, uh, bring your friend with you."

ARLIE SAT at the small police station, squeezing her fingers together in front of her. The officer sat down, sliding a cup of coffee to her.

"Nathan, what on earth are we going to do?" she asked, so thankful to have a familiar face to talk to. Granted, they were all pretty familiar, but Nathan had once been a family friend.

"Just stay calm," he said, squeezing her hand on top of the desk. "We're going to figure this out. Honestly, at this point, it could all be a coincidence."

"You've read my books, haven't you?"

He nodded. "Of course."

"How similar were they to what happened?"

He swallowed, looking away. "The things you wrote were...I mean, they could happen to anyone."

"But in order? And specifically like this? The chief's right. What if someone is trying to use my books to hurt people?"

"Relax, Arlie. Let's take this one step at a time, okay?

First of all, we need to know how you went about the research for your books. Did you talk to any experts?"

"Of course. I used you guys for a lot of the police procedural stuff, Google, and I went to Riverside and visited with some professors, too."

"The power of knowledge," he said with a smile. "Has anyone ever shown a particularly strong interest in your books?"

"I mean...I have fans, sure. From all over the world. I wouldn't say anyone was especially invested, but how would I know?" She shrugged, biting her nail.

"You've never been contacted by a fan?"

"Well, of course. Daily. I'm close to a lot of my fans. Internet-close, anyway. I have my Facebook reader's group and author page. I get emails daily. But my fans live all over the country. I don't think I have any die-hard fans here in Crimson Falls."

He touched a hand to his chest with a playful grin. "I'm offended."

"Okay, I have one," she said with a smirk. "Are you the killer?" She regretted the question as soon as she'd asked, realizing how tactless it was to make a joke like that.

Ignoring her question, he went on. "Have you ever received letters to your house from a fan? Or multiple emails? Anyone who came off to you as odd?"

"Well, I mean...not really. I've had to block some people on there. Ones who sent me email after email or wanted to video chat daily, whatever. But that's just Face-book. It's not anything to do with me." She paused, biting her lip and trying to think. Suddenly, a thought hit her. "Oh. But, I did have Roosevelt."

"Who's Roosevelt?"

"I'm pretty sure it was a fake name, but it's the only one he ever used. He was my...for lack of a better word... stalker. It was several years ago, before I was ever famous. Back when I first started writing. Roosevelt would write to me almost daily, sometimes more than once a day. In the beginning, it was normal. Like, telling me how much he liked my writing or he enjoyed a book. But then the emails got more demanding, asking me to meet him. Telling me how I should leave Brett and be with him. Telling me he could take care of me. He sent me letters to my house, pictures of my house, pictures of Brett and me, everything. It got really scary there for a while. I don't know why I didn't think of this before."

Nathan was taking notes as she spoke. "What happened to him?"

"I don't know," she said. "Brett and I...well, we spoke to the chief about it, filed a report and everything, but since he'd never truly threatened me, there wasn't a whole lot that could be done. Eventually, after months of no response, he just stopped writing. The pictures stopped coming. The chief said he must've gotten bored. I haven't heard from him in...two years? They stopped shortly before Brett passed."

Nathan nodded, flipping to a new page in his note-book. "Is there anything else you can think of that might help? Do you still have any of the old emails or photos?"

"Yes," Arlie said, "I have them all."

"Can I get you to send them to me?"

"Of course. Do you really think it could be him? Why would he do this? To get my attention, maybe? Why would he wait all this time?"

"I don't know," he said calmly. "But don't start

panicking yet. Just let us do some digging. In the meantime, you need to be extra cautious."

"Me? Why?"

"Because..." he said, looking at her as if it were obvious, "if the murderer is really a copycat, and he plans on acting out each of the book deaths, you'd be next, right? The next book is the one where a writer is killed?"

She swallowed hard. "Not the next one..." She trailed off, terror filling her. Could she really be in danger? "Wouldn't my number one fan know that?" She tried hard to fake a smile, though it just wasn't coming.

"I could've sworn it was." He touched his chin, staring at the ceiling as he tried to think.

"That's *The Girl Called Never*, and it's my last book. The next one is the homeless man, *The Goodbye Sister*."

"That's right," Nathan said, "I did know that."

"You don't really think any of this is true, do you? I mean, how crazy would someone have to be?"

"Just crazy enough," Nathan said, his voice low. "Speaking of, how well do you know this Mason guy?"

"Not well," she said honestly. "I only know what I told you guys before when I found him." She looked over her shoulder where Pete could be seen questioning Mason. "Why?"

"Well...a guy shows up on the outskirts of town, no one's ever seen or heard of him, he wasn't reported missing anywhere, and he claims he doesn't know who he is. It's just...it's odd. And then with all of this going on, it makes it even more...odd."

"Mason didn't have anything to do with this, Nathan. He's been with me. And he's not *claiming* not to know who he is, he genuinely doesn't. The doctor at the hospital even confirmed it."

"The doctor confirmed his memory loss?" he asked with a raised brow.

"Well, no," she said, looking down. "He said that wasn't possible. But he said that with the injuries sustained, it was possible, probable even, that he'd lose his memory."

"Arlie," Nathan said, leaning forward. "I don't trust him. I don't know what he wants from you, but I think you should ask him to leave. We can do that for you if it's easier."

"*No,*" Arlie insisted. "No. There's no reason for it. Mason wouldn't hurt anyone. And he's not asking me for anything. Everything I've given him has been because I wanted to. He's good, Nathan. I know sometimes it's hard to remember that good even exists outside of Crimson Falls, especially this time of year, but it does. And he is. He gave the Arbordale police his DNA and fingerprints. If he was a criminal, I'd think you would've had those results back by now."

"Not necessarily. You know how slow we are to get word here sometimes. And people commit crimes all the time without getting caught. Just because he's not in the system doesn't mean—"

"I trust him. That's all that matters." She pushed her chair back. "So, if that's all you need from me, I want to go home now."

Nathan closed his notebook. "Yeah, I guess that's all. For now. Just…you'll call me if you need anything, right?"

"You know I will," she said, offering up a sad smile.

"I mean anything," he said, staring at her with his piercing brown eyes. "And anytime. Day or night."

"I'll be fine, Nathan. I can take care of myself." With that, she turned, walking to where Mason sat. She was ready to go home.

CHAPTER TWELVE

Later that evening, Arlie and Mason sat at a corner booth in the diner at the edge of town. Arlie was picking at her plate of broccoli, trying to ignore her ever-growing headache. "I mean, it's crazy, right? It's got to be just a coincidence."

"I don't know," Mason said, taking a drink from his cup. "It's a pretty big coincidence if not."

"What do you think, then? Do you think I'm in danger?"

"No," he said quickly. "I would never let anything happen to you."

"You can't promise that, Mason. I can't let you put yourself at risk for me. Not when we don't know who we're up against."

"Hey," he whispered, taking her hand. "It's going to be okay."

"You don't understand. Tomorrow is October thirteenth. If anything bad is going to happen, it'll be tomorrow."

"But why?"

"It's Founders Day," she said, not wanting to explain.

"What's so bad about Founders Day? I know everyone here seems to be afraid of it, but it's just a day...right?"

"No," she said, her tone ominous. "Founders Day is cursed. Everything bad that happens in Crimson Falls happens around Founders Day. It's definitely not just another day."

He let out a stifled laugh.

"What?" she demanded.

"Oh, come on. *Cursed*? You can't be serious."

"I *am* serious, Mason. It's not a joke. Ask anyone. People here...they go crazy around Founders Day. It's dangerous. And now I've got a potential stalker to boot." She rubbed her forehead. "I should've never brought you here. Not now. It's not safe for you."

"Arlie," he said her name firmly, trying to get her to stop rambling, "I'm fine. You are going to be fine. We're going to make it through tomorrow, and you'll see that this is just all some insane coincidence. I promise you. I won't let anything happen to you. You don't have to protect me. I can take care of myself."

She shook her head. "That's what my husband thought, too. I begged him to stay home every Founders Day. But he never listened, and then he got cocky. He thought he was safe that day because he worked outside of Crimson Falls." She felt small tears forming in her eyes. "I can't lose anyone else...not after the way I lost him. I don't think I'll survive it."

He stood up, moving to her side of the booth and cradling her in his arms. "You aren't going to lose me. I'm here, okay?" he whispered, his lips moving against her ear. "I'm here, and I'm not going anywhere."

He pulled her away from him, kissing her softly. Her tears rubbed onto his skin, his hands in her hair, and for a moment—the first moment in a long time—she felt something in her heart telling her that maybe, just maybe, everything was going to be okay.

CHAPTER THIRTEEN

The next day, Arlie stood in the kitchen with her apron on. Mason's broad, muscled shoulders were practically on display under his thin, white T-shirt, and she couldn't help but admire him as he danced around the room with her. They'd turned the music up, locked the doors and windows, and created their own little place of solace. Nothing could penetrate their safe haven today. They wouldn't let it.

Mason looked up at her, noticing her stares, and smirked. "You're burning the pancakes," he teased, causing her to look down quickly, though he'd only been joking.

She scowled at him. "Just for that, I oughta burn yours."

He touched her shoulder with his forefinger, making a sizzling noise. "Oooh, ladies and gentleman, the girl is on fire."

She laughed, a loud belly laugh that felt foreign. "You are such a dork."

"But I'm *your* dork," he whispered, pulling her to him

suddenly and pressing his lips to hers. She wrapped her arms around his neck, ignoring the pancake batter that was probably splattered on him and the pancakes that probably *were* burning at this point.

She was safe with him. It was a foreign concept, but true nonetheless. This stranger, this man she hardly knew yet knew so well, was the only person she'd felt safe with for the past two years of her life. And he wanted her. He'd chosen her. Over his past life, or the pursuit of it. Over everything. Mason was hers, and she his.

There was no better feeling.

She'd never experienced a better October thirteenth. And after these twenty-four hours were over, they were going to continue on with their life. A new life. One they'd make together.

Interrupting her thoughts, her phone's shrill ring filled the house, and she immediately knew something was wrong. Something bad had entered their safe space. They weren't safe anymore. No matter how many locks they'd latched, nothing could bring them total safety. Of course not. She should've known. It was the one thing she'd always known. No one was safe on Founders Day.

Arlie pulled back from their kiss, the air between them suddenly ice cold. "Don't answer it," Mason begged.

"I have to," Arlie said, walking toward the living room with apprehension. She couldn't make out the name on the screen, though she knew who it would be. No one called her. No one had any reason to.

As she reached the couch arm, staring at the white letters that spelled 'Chief Chapman' but translated to 'trouble,' she picked up the phone with shaking hands, contemplating her next move.

With a deep breath, she slid her finger across the screen and placed the speaker to her ear. "Hello?"

Sigh. The familiar sigh that let her know her worst fears were being confirmed. "Arlie?"

She recognized the tone in his voice. A tone that could only bring bad news. "Yes?"

"We need you to come down to the station, sweetheart."

"What happened?"

"It's…Ted. He's…gone."

"Ted?" she asked, knowing who he must mean. Ted Daniels, the town drunk. "What happened?"

"Exactly what happened in your book," he said, his voice no longer soft. "He was stabbed to death last night. We found him this morning in an alley behind the Crimson Cafe."

"What?" she asked, covering her mouth. Without realizing he'd ever left the kitchen, Mason's arms were suddenly around her, his face soft as he seemed to realize who she must be talking to.

"It seems you two were at the diner last night around the time that he would've been killed."

"So someone really is after me?" she asked, thankful that Mason was beside her as her knees gave out under her.

"Well, that's one theory," he said with a sigh, "but I'm afraid there are others."

"Others? What do you mean?" She looked to Mason with worried eyes, and he squeezed her hand.

"I think it's best if you just come on down to the station, Arlie. We need to do this in person."

"Can I come tomorrow?" she asked. "With today being

what it is...we're trying to avoid town as much as possible."

He took a breath. "I'm sorry, Arlie. This really can't wait."

"Okay," she said, her voice little more than a squeak as she pressed her finger to the red button and looked up at Mason, fear in both of their eyes.

CHAPTER FOURTEEN

At the station once again, they immediately split Mason and Arlie. This time, the cop interviewing her was not Nathan, but rather the chief himself. The look on his face told her something was very wrong.

"I need you to tell me what you were doing at Crimson Cafe last night?"

"Um, I was…eating dinner with Mason."

"And what time did you leave?" he asked, taking notes as she spoke.

"I don't remember," she answered, picking at a loose piece of skin near her thumbnail. "Around eight or nine, I guess."

He stared at her. "It's really important that you remember, Arlie."

The way he said her name. Something was off, but she couldn't decide what. "It was closer to eight, I think."

He nodded. "And you went home with this…Mason?"

"I was with Mason, yes. He's still staying at my house."

"And were you with him the whole night?"

"Of course," she answered, though her cheeks grew pink with the answer.

"And he can confirm that?"

"Of course. Wait a second, you don't think Mason had anything to do with this, do you? You can't possibly believe that."

"To be honest, we aren't sure what to think."

"Meaning what?" She cocked her head to the side.

"Meaning whoever did this...whoever did all of this... has a surprisingly detailed knowledge of your books."

"What are you saying?" she asked, a lump suddenly in her throat.

"You know, Arlie, I don't want to think it's possible... but I have to ask."

"What exactly are you asking?" she asked, venom in her voice now as she stared at the betrayal written all over his face.

"I'm asking..." He pressed his lips together, rubbing a round finger over them. "Did you have something to do with this?"

"How can you ask that?" she demanded, standing from her chair. "Why on earth would I have anything to do with this? Because it's linked to my books? I'd have to be the world's dumbest serial killer, wouldn't I? What? You think I can't come up with new ideas? I'd just reuse the ones I already had? Seriously?" She was hyperventilating, furious and confused all at once. Was this what police work had come down to? Random assumptions and jumping to the easiest conclusions?

"Arlie, calm down," he said sternly.

"I can't calm down," she said. "Not if you seriously believe I could have *anything* to do with this. You've

71

known me since I was a kid, Reggie. Do you honestly believe I could...I could *kill* someone?"

He shook his head. "It's my job to ask the questions no one wants to ask. Believe me when I say I've been shocked more than once by what people are capable of. Especially on Founders Day. Just...just sit down. Let's talk. Get you cleared, and then we can move on and figure out who is actually behind this mess."

She sat down, her arms folded across her chest. "Okay," she said, though this was *so not okay.*

"So, Mason can confirm your whereabouts all night?"

"Yes."

"Good, that'll make this easy then. Has he started to remember anything?"

She shook her head. "No. No luck finding his family?"

He frowned, then closed his notebook. "No. Arlie, are you sure you're safe around him? I mean, what exactly do we know about him? Not even his name. He could be a criminal. He could be a killer. He could be insane."

"Oh, so you do think Mason had something to do with this, then? Why? Because he's not from here? Are we really that judgemental? He's not like us so he must be bad, is that it?"

He shook his head. "Don't forget who you're talking to, Arlie. I'm still the chief of police, whether I've known you since you were in diapers or not. And I'm not talking about him committing these murders in particular, though I'm certainly not ruling that out. How do you know he's not a stalker? If he did commit the murders, he could've targeted you. Maybe he's a crazed fan trying to get close to you, and you've just let him into your house. We haven't heard back about his fingerprints or DNA, but that doesn't mean they aren't there. And even if they aren't there, that doesn't mean he's not guilty of something. I'm only trying to protect you. He could be dangerous."

"He's nice to me," she said firmly. "He didn't find me. I found him. He didn't invite himself into my home. I did that. And he'd never even heard of me until I brought him home. He's not a stalker, Reggie. He's just a guy who needed help, and despite what this town has taught us… maybe there are actually people out there who are just…*good*, without any ulterior motive. Maybe there are places out there that don't go…freaking *Purge*-status once a year. This isn't normal, Reg. But Mason is. Mason is safe, not dangerous. *We* are the dangerous ones."

"I'm not accusing him of anything, Arlie. I'm asking. I'm trying to protect you because, yes, there are good people out there, but there are also really, really bad people out there."

She pushed her seat back again. "You think I don't know that? Do you even remember Brett?"

He closed his eyes, taking a moment before he spoke again. "I'm sorry. No. Of course I didn't forget him."

"I'm going to leave now." Her lips were pressed into a fine line as she strode toward the door. Without turning to face him, she placed her hand on the metal door knob. "Unless you're planning to hold me."

"No," his reply came, soft and low. "No, Arlie, of course not. Go on home. Just…just be careful out there, okay?"

Without another word, she pulled open the door and rushed from the room.

CHAPTER FIFTEEN

As Mason pulled the car into her driveway, Arlie's phone began buzzing. Her throat was dry, mind empty, as she removed her phone from her jacket pocket and stared at the screen.

She groaned. Phoebe was the last person she wanted to talk to at the moment. Especially considering that she'd made practically no progress on her manuscript since they'd last spoken.

"Hel—"

"Darling," Phoebe's shrill, joyful voice filled the line. "It's marvelous, isn't it? I mean, a tragedy, of course, but marvelous. Marvelous!" She let out a loud cackle. "Joey's called me twice this morning, numbers today are even better than yesterday. At this rate, you'll be hitting all the lists this week. Turns out, this little psycho was exactly what you needed to get back on top. And on top you are, honey. Muah." She made a kissing noise across the phone that made Arlie wrinkle her nose. The woman deserved an Oscar.

"What are you talking about?" she asked, her voice cracking.

"Oh, darling," Phoebe cried. "Haven't you been online? You're huge! Huge, Arlie. Bigger than before! Your books are on top of every chart." She giggled loudly. "It's *brilliant!*"

"What? Why?" she asked, sitting up straighter in the car's seat.

"Because…" Phoebe said, pausing for dramatic effect as she so often did. "Well, because of the…erm, *deaths*. The ones in that adorable little town of yours. You know, the murders that are happening just like the ones in your books."

Cold chills suddenly lined her arms. "How do you know about those?"

"Honestly, Arlie, it *is* okay to come out of the writer's cave for some fresh air every once in a while. Do you honestly not know what's been happening? You don't know about Bartholomew Danger?"

"Who's Bartholomew Danger?"

Phoebe cleared her throat. "He's…he's the man who's been chronicling the murders that have happened in your *quaint* little town. I have got to get down there one day, by the way. It seems so…quaint." She repeated the word. "We could do coffee. Or tea. Tea's very *in*, you know? Anyway, back to your success thanks to Bartholomew Danger. Bart. Barty. Seriously, darling, I assumed you knew. He's a blogger of some sort. Very small fish. But his blog has blown up lately. More specifically, when he started writing about you. Well, about the connections between the murders in your books and the murders that have occured. And, honestly, we're insanely lucky he did, because it's brought you back into the news. You're suddenly a hot topic again, Arlie. Your books are soaring, and people are just dying to get their hands on your new stuff. Which, I *know* you're making progress on."

"But who is he?" Arlie asked, ignoring her attempt to get information on the new book. "Someone who lives here in Crimson Falls?"

"I don't know. I wish I did. He only identifies himself as Bartholomew Danger. Very mysterious. His blogs are only so-so, but with a little help from the way your tales are spun, he is finding himself quite a little niche. Who knows, if we do find him, you owe him a hug. He's earning us both a big fat paycheck." With that, she laughed again.

Arlie placed a hand over her stomach, trying to calm it as it churned. "People are dead, Phoebe, you could show a bit of class here."

"Oh, dear," she said dramatically. "I'm sorry. You're right. I should. Of course, it *is* very sad. Honestly, it is. I hate it."

"Why are people so fascinated with death and tragedy? Fictional, sure, but real life tragedy? I just don't understand it."

"I don't know, love. But, I'm sorry to say, you should be glad they are. Seeing as how you seem to have built a career on it." Arlie sucked in a breath at her agent's harsh words, though Phoebe apologized again. "I'm sorry. I don't know why I said that. There I go, foot in mouth all over again. My mother always told me my mouth would get me into trouble. But, what can I say, it's also what's gotten me in a lot of doors. Betcha you're thankful for that, huh? Oh, look, there's my other line. I've got to go.

Listen, you just keep writing. I'll take care of the rest." With that, the line clicked and Arlie pulled the phone from her ear.

"What was that about?" Mason asked, staring at her with a worried expression.

"It was my agent," she said with a sigh. "Bad news is, people are dying. Good news, that seems to have catapulted my career. *Again.*" She closed her eyes, feeling cool tears well in them. "Why does this keep happening to me?"

He wrapped an arm around her, pulling her into his shoulders. "Shhh," he soothed. "It's going to be okay."

"No." She sobbed. "No, it's not. Nothing is going to be okay because…tragedy follows me. And it's never going to stop following me. And somehow I'm supposed to be grateful because good seems to come from all of the bad in my life, but I'm not grateful. I'd give up every ounce of the good for the bad to just go away." She was rambling. Sobbing and snotting all over Mason's new shirt, but he didn't seem to care. His strong arms surrounded her, keeping her safe. Or, at least, attempting to. They sat in the car for what seemed like hours, him holding her and allowing her to cry for as long as she needed. Mason was the only person who seemed to understand. The only person who cared to understand. And none of this was his fault. He'd been dragged into her mess. And now he was a suspect in this crazy web. It was all her fault, and she wasn't sure what to do to save him. Because she had to save him. She needed to. She needed him.

She pressed her face into his chest more fully, realizing just how much she needed him and just how much that terrified her. At the end of the day, Mason mattered to her. More than she'd probably realized. More than she'd ever admit to him. She had to figure out a way to fix this.

When she'd calmed slightly, she pulled away, wiping her tears. "I'm sorry."

"You don't have to be—"

"No, I do. I'm sorry I dragged you into all of this."

"You saved my life."

"Or maybe I ruined it."

He clasped her shoulders, lowering his head so he was eye level with her. "Hey," he said firmly. "You haven't ruined anything. You saved me. You were kind to me. You didn't have to be. You didn't have to do anything, but you did. You're a good person, Arlie. And I'm sorry that all of this darkness seems to surround you. I wish I could do something to take it all away."

She closed her eyes, nodding her head. "Do you really mean that?"

"Of course I do," he insisted. "Just name it. I'd do anything to help you. I owe you everything."

"You might regret saying that," she said, placing her head on his chest again. "Because I actually could use your help with something."

CHAPTER SIXTEEN

Inside the house, Arlie was on her laptop, Mason at her side. "If we can find out who this Bartholomew Danger is, we can confront him. See what he knows. How he knows it. Maybe if we do that, we can figure out who's doing this. If we solve the murders, or at least point the police in the right direction, they'll finally believe we're innocent and then we can try to move on."

"Okay, so how do we find him?" he asked, reading over her shoulder as she pulled up the first blog post that appeared from her search.

She gasped as she read through the gruesome blog, filled with more details than the police had given her. So, how then could this blogger, this Bartholomew Danger, possibly know all of this? It had to be someone from Crimson Falls. As she read on, flipping through daily posts about the crimes, posts asking questions she wanted answers to herself, she found herself growing angrier. Just who was this person? Was he the killer? How did he know what he knew? And what gave him the right to publish it?

What gave him the right to make a spectacle of her life? To make a spectacle of so many deaths. These people deserved more. She deserved more.

She clicked on the HOME button, going to the homepage of the website where Bartholomew's blog was hosted. It was true what Phoebe said. He'd been blogging for a few years about random things: book reviews, recipes, updates on his pet Yorkie. But it was only recently, since he'd started blogging about her, about her town, and about the deaths that were rocking it, that he had begun to gain traction. Suddenly, the blogs were filled with comments—speculations, questions, people claiming they were reading her books to find the similarities, people claiming she must be guilty, people claiming Bartholomew himself must be guilty. She flipped through the page, searching for a way to contact him. There must be a way. And yet, she couldn't find it. No contact form, no email address. Bartholomew Danger did not want to be found. But, Arlie Montgomery did not like to give up.

She went back to the search engine, typing in his name. There were no Bartholomew Dangers. No real ones anyway. She flipped through pages and pages of his blog posts, looking for him on Facebook to no avail. What kind of blogger wasn't on Facebook? She looked at the avatar on his website. Dark hair, glasses, bright green eyes. Could this be what he looked like? After all, we are all better versions of ourselves online. Perhaps he was overweight or acne ridden. Perhaps he was none of those things. She might never know.

She closed the computer. "Do you think the police know about this? I mean, we could take this to them. Tell them to look him up. They can check his IP address or whatever, right?"

"I don't know, Arlie. I don't know how any of it works, honestly. They could just think we're chasing our tails."

"Is that what you think?" she asked, staring up at him. She needed his honesty. She needed it more than she could possibly explain in that moment. Was she crazy? Was she grasping at straws? Was she hoping so badly to point the blame at someone else that she was being ridiculous? Because the person they believed could be behind it—the person they believed could be guilty—she couldn't stomach the possibility. It wasn't Mason. It couldn't be. She created Mason. He was perfect. He was beautiful. He was hers. And most importantly, he was innocent.

"I don't know, Arlie," he answered finally. "I really don't. For all we know, this blogger is just some sick kid who's fascinated with death."

"But what if he's not? What if he actually is the killer?"

"Then we wait," he said firmly. "We make it through today, and we let the cops do their jobs. I will keep you safe. You know that. We both know we're innocent. That's what matters right now, okay?"

She nodded, not feeling entirely sure she agreed. Everything else seemed to matter. The truth seemed to matter. Bringing the bad guys to justice seemed to matter. But she wasn't in the mood to argue. She didn't have the energy for it. Murder investigation was completely exhausting, truth be told. So, instead, she waited for Mason to stand up, making his way over to light the gas fireplace. "Let's just relax. We'll find a good movie. I'll start something for supper. All of our problems will be here tomorrow."

Arlie nodded, though she quickly copied the URL of Bartholomew Danger's blog and pasted it into an email. She typed the chief's email address and pressed send before closing the laptop, trying to hide her worried grin.

CHAPTER SEVENTEEN

They'd made it through the day. Arlie heaved a sigh. She had no returned email from the chief, but she also hadn't heard anything else about any murders. The day was coming to a close, and she was safe. She sat on the couch alone as she heard Mason heading back down the hallway.

He rubbed a towel through his wet hair. "You okay?" he asked, noticing her blank stare at the wall.

She turned to face him, shaking her head to brush off the trance she'd been in. "Sorry, I'm fine. Just...tired, I guess."

"I can't say that I blame you there." He glanced at the clock. "Only two more hours left in the day. We made it."

"Don't jinx us," she said firmly, though she'd just been thinking the same thing. "What about tomorrow?"

He sank into the couch next to her, an arm around her shoulders. His breath was minty, and he smelled of men's soap. He was clean and new, and she smelled of staleness and the police station. He leaned his head over onto hers.

"Tomorrow is a new day. We'll be together. That's all that matters, right?"

She nodded, turning to face him. She ran a finger over his wound, tracing the outline. The closer it grew to being healed, the more she was reminded that someday soon his memory would be healed, too. And then this would all be over. And he'd leave her. And she'd be all alone again.

Seeming to read her mind, he reached up, touching her fingers lightly. "I'm fine," he whispered, kissing her nose. "We're fine." He pulled her fingers to his mouth, kissing them carefully. "Everything's going to be fine."

She stared into his eyes, wondering if it were even possible that it could've been true. As if to answer her question, her phone began buzzing in the pocket of her robe. She reached into it, pulling it out and checking the screen. It was the chief. She stood, making her way to the window before putting the phone to her ear.

"Hello?" she asked.

"Arlie, it's Chief Chapman."

"I know," she said softly. "Is everything okay?"

"Where are you right now?"

"At home."

"Is *he* there?" the chief asked.

"Mason?" she asked, turning around to glance at him. She stopped short. He was gone, his imprint still in the couch.

"Yes, Mason. Listen, Arlie, I checked into that article you sent me. I checked the IP address."

"Okay, and?" she asked, peeking around the corner of the hall to check for him.

"I'm sending Nathan to your house now to pick him

up, Arlie. Do you hear me? It was him. We think it was Mason."

The words hit her like a block of ice square to the chest, sending cold chills down her body. "What are you talking about?"

"Has he had access to your computer? Any computer in your house?"

"Um, I don't know, I guess so. Why? What are you talking about?" She recalled walking into her office when she'd caught him on the computer, though he'd had a valid reason to be using it. He hadn't been trying to hide anything...but he did shut the computer quickly. She remembered that.

"The connection, Arlie. It was coming from inside your house."

Someone was moving in the kitchen. Slow, methodical footsteps. She slid her phone back into her pocket without another word, but without pressing the end button. "Mason?" she called, searching for his face. As she made her way into the kitchen, someone grabbed her hair. She closed her eyes seconds before her face made contact with the counter and then...it all went black.

CHAPTER EIGHTEEN

Arlie awoke to flashing lights. No, wait. That was her eyes opening and closing. Where was she? What was happening? Her eyes were dry, and she seemed incapable of keeping them open for longer than a few seconds. She moved to rub them, but something stopped her. Something was pulling at her skin.

She turned her head slowly, noticing the stiffness, and opened her eyes again. The bed she was in was not her own. It was white. Crisp. Too clean. She stared down at the IV line taped to her arm. It took a moment before she realized where she was. A hospital. In Arbordale or River- side, she couldn't be sure. Her whole face was a giant bruise, every new expression causing her pain. She tried to sit up in bed, but a noise outside of her room stopped her. She watched the metal door handle twist. Someone was coming.

As the door opened and a doctor appeared, his salt and pepper hair and warm, friendly smile caused a memory to come back to her. *Mason.* Where was Mason? The chief had said he was guilty. Could that be true?

"Well, Arlie, it's great to see that you're awake," the doctor said, looking at the machine above her bed before typing something into the iPad in his hands. "How are you feeling?"

"Sore," she said honestly, her voice throaty. "Am I... what happened?"

"You're going to be fine," he assured her, taking a seat in the chair next to her bed. He placed a hand on her arm cautiously. "I'm Doctor Ryan. It's nice to officially meet you."

"What happened to me?" she asked again. "Did someone try to hurt me?"

"Someone did," he said. "You were...attacked, Arlie. In your home. You were lucky to have survived. The police brought you here. You've got a broken nose that we've reset and a lot of bruising, but you're going to be okay."

"Who...do they know who it was? Who hurt me?"

"I'm afraid you'll have to talk to the cops about that. But not to worry, okay? You're safe here. In fact, the officer who found you has your room guarded. I can send him in if you'd like."

"Please," Arlie said, nodding her head cautiously. "I have to know the truth."

"Sure," the doctor said, standing from his chair. "Is there anything you need right now? I can have one of the nurses get you a drink, maybe? It's past dinner time, but we could get a snack brought up if you're hungry."

"A drink would be great," she said, touching her parched throat for emphasis.

"You've got it." He bowed out of the room quickly, and within seconds it was opening again.

Nathan stood in front of her, and in that moment, she was so grateful to see a familiar face she could've cried. "Nathan," she said, tears in her eyes.

"Arlie, thank God you're okay," he said, rushing to her side. "I was so worried about you."

"What happened?" he asked.

"I was hoping you could tell me."

"You mean you don't know?"

"I...I remember being at home. With Mason," she watched the officer's eyes go stony as she said his name, but went on, "but I don't remember much else."

"Do you remember the email you sent the chief about Bartholomew Danger?"

She nodded, the memory coming back slowly. "I do."

"And the phone call he made to you?"

"About the IP address," she said quickly. "Yes. I do. I do remember."

"I was already on my way to you when he called. He said he heard you put your phone down." He was speaking through partially gritted teeth, his jaw tight. "And then you screamed. When I got there, you were in the floor. And the blood...there was so much blood. I thought you were dead."

"I'm fine, Nathan," she said calmly.

"I know," he said, nodding and looking away. "I'm glad. But we arrested Mason. Or whatever his name is. He's down at the station now being interrogated. If you could remember what happened, we can make sure he can never hurt you again."

She shook her head, tears forming in her eyes once

again. She tried to scrape the fuzzy memory from her mind. *Someone* had been in the kitchen. *Someone* had grabbed her hair and shoved her into the countertop. *Someone.* But she couldn't be sure it was Mason.

"I don't know," she said finally. "I can't…I can't remember. They…he attacked me from behind. I never saw the person. Not that I can remember."

"Are you remembering clearly?"

"I don't know."

"Was anyone else in the house with you?"

She looked down, folding her hands together again and again. "No. It was just the two of us."

"When we found Mason, he was in the restroom. Washing his hands. Probably washing away evidence of the crime. *Your* blood, Arlie. You have to remember. Without your testimony, this psycho could walk."

She closed her eyes. "I don't want to believe it."

"I know, but—"

She held up her hand to stop him. "I don't want to believe it, but I guess it's true." His face was coming back to her. The blurry outline of him as he walked away. Maybe it had been him. It had to have been. Who else was there? "I can sort of remember it now. It's just…it's hard. I trusted him."

"I know you did," he said calmly, patting her hand. In his pocket, a phone started ringing and he stood up. Her heart pounded as she watched him walk to the edge of her room, but to her relief he didn't leave. "Chief." He paused. "Mhm…no shit? Mhm, okay. Okay, yes I'm with her. Okay. Do you need me to…okay. Thanks." He lowered the phone from his ear, slipping it back into his jacket pocket and turning back around. His head hung, his eyes not meeting hers as he walked back toward her.

"What is it?" she asked.

"The police searched your house. Looking for anything that might incriminate Mason further."

She swallowed. "Did they find anything?"

"They did," he said, meeting her eyes finally.

"They found the murder weapons. The gun from Perry's death and the knife from Ted's."

"It was him," she said, letting out a slow, agonizing breath. "He really did those horrible things? He *killed* those people?" She'd had a killer in her house. In her bed. In her body. She'd let a killer into her life. She'd kissed a killer. She'd *fucked* a killer. Oh. What had she done? Her heart pounded, her breathing growing erratic as the machine next to her beeped loudly.

"There's more," Nathan said, sitting down next to her once again. "They found a wallet."

"A wallet? He robbed someone?"

"No. The wallet was his. Or should I say...it was Alec Hopewood's."

Hopewood. *No.*

CHAPTER NINETEEN

BEFORE

"Hello, beautiful," Brett said, kissing his wife's neck from behind. She jumped at his touch, turning around and slapping him playfully.

"Way to scare a girl," she said, kissing him back.

"I thought you liked being scared." He wiggled his eyebrows before pointing his nose to the ceiling like a bloodhound. "Smells delicious. What are you cooking?"

"Shrimp scampi." She turned back to the pan, grabbing a piece of shrimp on a fork and offering it to him. He took a bite slowly.

"As delicious as it is," he whispered, his eyes dancing over her, "it's not as delicious as you look."

"Easy, boy. Our guests will be here any minute."

"We have time," he promised, pressing his body against hers.

"I don't think so. Not if you don't want dinner burnt."

He took another bite, kissing her lips. "I told you pizza was fine with me."

"Pizza is not what you serve dinner guests."

"We live in Crimson Falls, love. I don't think anyone is

expecting a four-course meal." He snapped his fingers. "Oh, speaking of guests. Take off the 's.'"

"What? Why?"

"Her husband had a thing. Work or whatever."

"Well, shouldn't we reschedule? I mean, isn't the whole point of a double date to have two couples here?" She offered up a playful smile, though her heart was sinking.

"No. No, it's fine. Meaghan didn't want to trouble us. She knew you'd be cooking, and there's no reason for it to go to waste. The four of us can get together again another time."

"Won't it be awkward for her, though?"

He let out a sigh, his forehead wrinkling. She took her thumb and moved to smooth it out as she so often did. "We'll just have to make sure it isn't," he said, kissing her again before heading from the room. He was already unbuttoning his shirt when the doorbell rang. "Honey, could you get that? I'm going to run and change."

She nodded, pulling the pan from the stovetop and setting her oven mitt down. She dusted off her apron, glancing at the clock. Meaghan was early. She walked to the door cautiously, pulling it open and forcing a smile.

Meaghan was small, in every sense of the word. A petite brunette with a tiny waist, eyes a bit too close together and lips that were chapped. Despite her flaws, she was gorgeous. And young. Enough to make Arlie hesitate.

"Hi," she said with a large grin. She held out a bottle of wine. Red when she should've brought white. If she'd bothered to ask what they were having, she could've paired them appropriately, but whatever. "You must be Arlie."

"I am," Arlie said, finally out of her trance. She stepped back. "Come on in. Brett's just run to change clothes."

"Thank you so much for having me over. I hope you aren't

too thrown off by my husband not coming. He had a work thing." She raised her eyebrows, looking away. "You know how it is."

"Oh, no. That's okay. I'm sure the four of us can get together another time." She was echoing her husband's words, not entirely paying attention to what was being said as she watched the girl taking in their home. Was it too small? Not as well decorated as she'd imagined? Nothing like she was used to? Did she think Arlie must be a horrible housekeeper? That Brett deserved better? Arlie shook her head. She was being ridiculous. The girl was married. And half their age. She wasn't a threat to her. Besides that, Brett loved her. He loved her. She was safe.

"I am just so excited to meet you," she said, and Arlie detected a hint of Southern twang. "Brett has told me so much about you, but I'm never out this way. Riverside's not that far, but honestly Arbordale is the furthest I ever go, and that's just for work."

"You're from Riverside?"

"Yeah," she said, smiling at Brett as he walked into the room. "Hey you." She reached out to hug him, and Brett obliged awkwardly, his eyes on Arlie.

"I thought you lived in Arbordale," Arlie said.

"No, honey," Brett told her, "I told you Meaghan was from Riverside, didn't I?"

"No, I don't think so."

"What? Is there a turf war?" Meaghan joked. "Am I wearing the wrong color?"

Arlie shook her head, wrapping an arm around her husband to pull him to her side. "No, of course not." She laughed. "It's just...I wish you hadn't had to drive so far to come. We could've all met in Arbordale if I'd known."

"It's all right. I just came straight from work, actually.

Which is why I look so terrible. Excuse my appearance." She was fishing for a compliment, and though Arlie knew it and refused to offer one, Brett didn't seem to be aware of her resistance.

"You look fine," he told her, reaching out to take the wine from her grasp. "Make yourself comfortable. Should I open this?"

He looked to Arlie, who nodded uncomfortably. Should she point out that white would go better with the dish? She decided against it. "Dinner is almost ready. I'll get the table set."

Meaghan sat down on the couch, crossing her legs so that her skirt rode up even further, and Arlie followed Brett into the kitchen. He grabbed three glasses from the cabinet and poured their drinks. His gaze never met Arlie's, though she tried desperately to catch his eye. Something was off about him. Suddenly he was one of those guys. He was all too charming. His act was done well, but Arlie could see through it. She knew her husband. This was not him. If it were one of the guys, they would've met them closer. If it were one of the guys, and their wives couldn't make it, they would reschedule. So what was it about Meaghan that made Brett suddenly lose his nerve?

She knew what it was. She'd known what it was the second she saw the tight skirt and perky breasts. The fake smile.

This girl was vindictive. Young. She made Arlie self-conscious, something she'd hardly felt before. Brett loved her. She knew that. But something about this felt off.

She placed the food on their plates quietly as Brett disappeared into the living room with two glasses. She could hear them laughing and carrying on, and as her anger bubbled, she took a deep breath.

She was being ridiculous. This was Brett. He wasn't capable of an affair. He loved her too much.

She set the plates on the table, laying out the silverware and taking off her apron as she walked into the living room. She tried to ignore the way Brett's hand left Meaghan's arm the second she appeared.

"Dinner's ready." She felt more like a maid than a wife, hating herself for the unfounded jealousy filling her chest. She was not a jealous person. What on earth was happening to her?

"Perfect, I'm starving. It smells delicious, Arlie." Meaghan stood, waiting for Brett to lead the way, and Arlie fell behind them. Brett pulled out the chair at the head of the table, waiting for the ladies to take a seat on either side of him before he sat down.

"This looks amazing, babe," Brett said, squeezing her hand. Arlie smiled at him.

"Thank you." She took a drink of the wine. A gulp, more like it. It was going to be a long night.

AFTER DINNER WAS OVER, *Arlie was cleaning the dishes as Brett and Meaghan remained at the table, their laughter echoing throughout the small room. Arlie cast sideways glances at them, her hands raw from how hard she was scrubbing, but everything she did seemed to go unnoticed by her husband.*

When she had finished, she dried her hands on the towel that hung by the stove, laying it on the countertop and refilling her glass of wine. She was on her fourth glass. Or maybe her fifth. And it was finally white wine, which would've actually gone nicely with the meal she'd slaved over.

What did it matter? Brett and Meaghan had hardly touched their glasses, so lost in each other. She walked toward them, merely feet away when Brett finally noticed. "Hello, darling. Sit down," he said. "You look exhausted." He patted the table as if she were supposed to sit there.

"I am," she said. "It's getting late." It was a hint to Meaghan, and her gaze fell to her. "Don't you think?"

"Yes, of course," Brett answered. "Why don't you go on up to bed. I'll finish cleaning up down here."

She looked around at the spotless kitchen, ignoring the urge to roll her eyes. "I was just thinking Meaghan should get going. It's getting late, after all. You have a long drive home."

"Honey—" Brett started, his voice tight.

"It's okay," Meaghan said, and Arlie let out a sigh of relief as she stood. "She's right. I didn't notice the time. I should get going. Arlie, thank you so much for having me here tonight. I had a lot of fun. We'll have to do it again."

"Yes," Arlie lied, "we'll have to." She accepted the stiff hug Meaghan offered her.

"I'll walk her out," Brett said, kissing his wife's cheek. "You get upstairs and wait for me." His hand slid down her back, nearly touching her butt, but stopping. Her cheeks flamed at his touch. "I'll be right back."

Arlie nodded. "Drive safe," she told Meaghan before turning and heading for the bedroom.

As she entered, she immediately stripped out of her dress, pulling her silk robe out of a drawer and tying it around herself. She pulled the pins from her hair, letting the brown curls fall loose. As she searched through her makeup, looking for her favorite red lipstick, she remembered she had left it in the bathroom. She opened the door, tiptoeing out across the hall to grab it. She grabbed the lipstick from the blue countertop, turned back around, and stopped. The lipstick fell to the floor, its plastic colliding loudly with the linoleum.

She let out a haggard breath, staring at her husband, his lips *red from Meaghan's own lipstick, his hands wrapped around her waist. Meaghan's lips formed a perfect 'O' as she stepped away from Brett. "I'm so sorry." She darted out the door without another word, and Arlie sank to the floor, tears muddling her vision as she attempted to clean the broken lipstick from the floor.*

Brett rushed toward her. Her, not Meaghan. "Arlie."

She stood up, staring at him with a hate-filled expression. She waited for him to explain. To say anything. But he didn't. His eyes lined with tears of his own.

"How long?" she asked, the words barely escaping her throat.

"What?" he asked.

"How long has it been going on?" Her teeth were bared, her body filled with adrenaline.

"It hasn't...nothing's—"

"How long have you been screwing her?" *she screeched.*

"I..." He let out a sigh, looking down. "About a month."

She nodded, tossing the broken lipstick into a nearby trash can and walking to the sink again to wash her hands. He approached her, meeting her eyes in the mirror. "I'm sorry. I don't know what I was thinking. She means nothing to me."

"Did you get that line from the Cheater's 101 Handbook? The chapter about what lie to use when you get caught?" She'd known. Somehow in her gut, the moment she'd seen Meaghan, she'd just known. It explained the jealousy. It was why the night had been miserable for her. As much as she wanted to believe she'd been wrong, somehow...she'd just known.

He lowered his head again, his forehead on her shoulder, but she bumped him off. "I should've told you sooner."

"You shouldn't have done it," she said, slamming her hands onto the sinktop.

"I know. I shouldn't have. I wish I hadn't."

"Are you still planning to see her? Do you want to divorce me?"

"No! No, of course not. I'll have her let go. Fired. Honestly, she's not that great of an assistant anyway. I don't want to lose you. I still love you so much. I was stupid. This was all so stupid."

"Why would you bring her here?"

"Honestly, I don't know. I thought if the four of us could get together...I don't know." He crossed his arms. "I don't know why I did it. I don't have a reasonable explanation."

"Was I just a joke to you? Were the two of you joking around all night about your little secret? While I'm just here playing dutiful wife?" She wiped her tears as quickly as they fell, her body shaking with anger.

"Of course not." He pulled her into a hug and she didn't resist. "Of course not. I love you, Arlie. You. Not her. I never loved her. Meaghan was just...I don't know. I've been so stressed at work. It was stupid." He pulled her away from his chest, holding her shoulders so she would look at him. "I was stupid. It's over. I just don't want to lose you."

"I want her gone," she said through gritted teeth.

"Done." He nodded in agreement.

"Have there been others?"

"No," he answered quickly. "No."

"Good," she said with a deep breath. She pulled away from his grasp and walked past him. "Now come to bed."

She laid in bed, feeling his body next to hers, the covers rising and falling with his every breath, but she couldn't sleep. She cried silent tears, feeling so disgusted with him and with herself. She picked apart every piece of her body and her life, comparing herself to Meaghan over and over and over. She wondered if she'd ever be able to sleep again.

CHAPTER TWENTY

The day of the shooting, October 13th, 2016, was nearly a year since news of Brett's affair had broken. Meaghan had been fired the day after she'd come to dinner, and Arlie and Brett's marriage had been repaired, slowly, through intense counseling and hard work. He was back to writing her love letters. He brought home flowers just because. She was back in the gym three times a week, trying to keep herself perfect for the husband she loved more than life. She didn't trust him completely yet, and their counselor said that was normal. It would take time. Brett had to earn her trust again. Earn her forgiveness. But he was trying. God knew he was trying, and that was all she could ask for. Actually, she could've asked for a husband who hadn't cheated at all, but the counselor said those thoughts wouldn't help matters. What was done was done, and there was nothing else she could do but move forward. She still loved him, and he never stopped loving her. That was the truth. And that was what mattered.

It was at the gym where she'd heard news of what had happened. Lauren Alberts had run up to her on the elliptical, *her eyes filled with tears. "Arlie," she cried, falling onto her before Arlie had stopped running. Lauren's husband worked with Brett in Arbordale.*

"What is it?" she asked, hugging her friend.

"It's...there was a shooter." Her words were muffled against Arlie's shoulders, her body shaking with her sobs. Arlie patted her head, trying to pull her hair away from her face so she could hear.

"A what?"

"A shooter," Lauren said again. "At Dunlin-Hammel." Arlie's blood ran cold, and she shook her friend.

"Who was it? Was anyone hurt?" Cold chills lined her arms.

"I don't know," Lauren cried. The girls sank to the floor together, their sobs echoing through the quiet gym. People around them stopped exercising, hurrying to their sides to see what had happened.

Arlie didn't remember much of the next few moments, even now, but it didn't matter. Brett was gone. She could feel it in her bones. When she collected herself enough to find her phone, she dialed his number. Again and again and again. Over and over until she'd left him so many messages his inbox was full. She couldn't even hear his voice anymore. She drove to Arbordale but wasn't allowed near his building. Police barricaded the streets as they led the shooter out of the building.

A disgruntled ex-employee who would serve a life sentence being taken care of by the government. Three meals a day while her husband rotted in the ground. A bed and television while her husband would never again laugh at Kevin James' comedy. She watched as the ambulances loaded up body after body. So many dead. So many killed by the monster.

Finally, a policeman walked up to her, noticing her sobs as the hysteria of the event seemed to calm down.

"Did you...did you know someone in the building?" he asked, his eyes soft.

"My husband." She nodded. "My husband, Brett Montgomery. He...I can't get him to answer his phone."

The cop nodded, placing a hand on her shoulder after he'd jotted down the name. "I'll see what I can find out."

Tears poured down her face as the policeman went to talk to a few of the other officers working the scene. They'd begun to talk to witnesses, walking them out of the building once the gunman had been driven off. Arlie watched the door open, but she couldn't believe what she was seeing.

There, spattered in blood—Brett's blood, she would later find out—was Meaghan Hopewood, the woman her husband swore to have fired just one year ago.

A rlie walked into the prison a month later, her hands clenched into fists. She was led by a guard to a room eerily like the ones she'd seen on TV. It was gray and smelled damp and had a long row of red chairs facing the glass that led to the other side. The side where the prisoners would sit. The side where Mason would be waiting. As she walked down the long room, she finally laid eyes on him. He looked different. His head was shaven, his blue eyes darker somehow. His head wound had healed up, though he had different lacerations on his face now. He hadn't had it easy in here, that much was clear.

She sat down across from him, picking up the heavy, black phone and placing it to her ear.

He put a hand on the glass, his palm reaching for hers. She didn't return his advance. "Hey," he said softly, his voice incredibly clear in her ear.

"Hey," she whispered, her voice echoing in the too-quiet room. There was a sign to her left that said 'Please

Keep Hands Visible at all Times,' and she untucked her hand from under her elbow instantly. "How are you?"

He looked down, shaking his head. "I'm okay...you know, as good as can be expected. My lawyer...he, uh, he told me who I am. That you found a wallet."

"We shouldn't be discussing the case," she warned him.

"Is it true?" He pressed on. "I was married? I had a wife? And she worked with your husband?"

She nodded, though she didn't dare speak. "Your lawyer will take care of you, Mason. Er, I guess I should call you Alec now, huh?"

"I still feel more like Mason." He shook his head. "They have doctors in here. Trying to heal my memory, but I don't know if I want that. They've tried to contact my wife...but she isn't answering. Do you think you could reach out to her? My lawyer said it may help if I have someone...you know, family, in court."

"I don't think so," she said, running a quick finger over her lip.

He closed his eyes. "Of course not. Why would you help me? You probably hate me."

"I don't hate you."

"I didn't do it," he said, his voice raised as his hand went back to the glass. His eyes pleaded with her. "I swear to you I didn't. I would never hurt you, Arlie. I would never hurt anyone. I care about you. I'm so glad you're safe. I need you to know that. No matter what happens, I need to know you believe I'm innocent. You're the only person I feel like I can trust right now. And, you can trust me. I would *never* do anything to hurt you. Never." He pressed his fingers to his temples. "My lawyer is trying to work up an insanity plea. He says it may be my best option. With my injury," he pointed to his head, "he says we have a pretty good chance. But, even with that, it's likely I'll never make it out. I can survive that, if I have to. But I can't survive it if I think you believe I could be guilty. I can't."

She nodded. "I really don't think we should be discussing it."

"I know," he agreed. "I just…I didn't do it. I need you to believe me. I need to hear you say you believe me."

She took a breath, pressing her mouth further into the phone. "I do."

"You do?" he asked, his eyes lighting up at her words.

"I do believe you. I know you didn't do this."

Tears lined his eyes, and he wiped them away with dirty fingers. "Thank God. You have no idea what that means to me."

She pushed her chair back, suddenly overwhelmed with her surroundings. "Just…just take care of yourself, okay?"

"Wait!" he called, causing her to stop. "Would you tell the police that? Would you be willing to testify for me? I need you to tell them that I wasn't the one who hurt you. That evidence…it must've been planted. It wasn't mine."

"I know," she repeated, nodding her head and leaning closer to the glass. "But I can't."

"You can't?"

"I can't tell anyone." Her voice was firm. Much more confident than she felt. "I'm sorry."

"What do you mean?" he demanded, hitting the glass. "Why can't you?"

"Because." She closed her eyes. "Because I need for it to have been you." With that, she placed the phone back into place and turned away from him, despite his pleading. Her heels clicked down the long room as she disappeared, trying desperately to ignore his cries.

What she'd said was true, no matter how much it hurt. *It had to be him.*

CHAPTER TWENTY-TWO

BEFORE

Arlie sat in her car outside of the hospital's morgue. She stared at the bag of her husband's things. His phone. His blazer. His wallet. The last things he'd touched. The last things he'd ever wear. She held the bag tightly, loud, obnoxious sobs escaping her throat. How dare he? How dare he leave her like this? How dare he die for Meaghan?

The police had told her what the witnesses said, though Meaghan had never come around. They'd told her how multiple people said Brett jumped in front of Meaghan, pushed her to the ground. His body was a shield that kept her alive. In the end, he chose her. He chose to save her over a life with his wife.

Everyone kept telling her how much of a hero he was, how she should feel so proud of him, that his last act was so noble. But it didn't feel noble. It felt like betrayal. He'd left her. He'd lied to her. All this time...he'd never ended things with Meaghan, never fired her. And she'd just blindly trusted him. She'd never asked questions, never stopped by his office unannounced, never checked his email or phone.

Phone.

Thinking quickly, she opened the bag, pulling his phone from it and trying to ignore the dried blood against the black Otterbox. She typed in his password, their anniversary, and clicked on the green messages icon.

She didn't have to look far. There, right in front of her eyes, were messages upon messages from Meaghan. Good night texts. Good morning texts. I love you texts.

He loved her.

She loved him.

That truth struck her hard.

Her husband loved a woman that wasn't her. They texted almost incessantly. All the times that he'd claimed to be dealing with 'work,' it seemed as though they were all her. She closed out of the messages, gasping for air, and despite her better judgement, opened his pictures.

You know the old saying about curiosity and the cat? Well, Arlie could feel her whiskers growing as she waited for the death the pictures on his phone were sure to bring her. The pictures of herself and Brett were scarce compared to the pictures he had of Meaghan and himself.

Naked selfies she'd sent him, pictures of the two of them in bed together, pictures of them out on dates, at the park. Pictures of them kissing. She stopped on a picture of the two of them in a bed that she didn't recognize. It must've been Meaghan's. She was kissing his forehead and he had a goofy grin on his face.

He was happy. She could see it. There was a light in his eyes she hadn't realized she'd been missing for quite a while. She wasn't sure when it had disappeared.

Somehow, foolishly, she'd always believed he was happy with her. Their sex life wasn't perfect, but it certainly wasn't stale. He still kissed her goodbye every morning. Still called her beautiful every night.

So where had she gone wrong? And what could she ever do with this information? She contemplated sending the pictures to Meaghan's husband, if she could manage to track him down, but what was the point?

Brett was gone, and she was alone.

In his final moments, he had been holding another woman.

A woman that he loved.

A woman that wasn't her.

CHAPTER TWENTY-THREE

*S*ix *months after Brett's death, a knock sounded on Arlie's door. Arlie stared at the shadow behind the blind, wondering who it could be. Who would be visiting her? She had no family to speak of. Her only living relative was her mother, and it wasn't like the nursing home she was in allowed her to make trips back home.*

She stood up, making her way to the door and peeking out the curtain. The sight of Meaghan standing in front of her caused her to gasp. Meaghan looked her way at the sound, squinting her eyes as she strained to see through the glass.

"Arlie?" she called, leaning forward.

For a second, Arlie considered closing the blind and walking away. She had absolutely nothing to say to this woman. The woman who was responsible for the end of her husband's life.

Okay, that may have been a slight exaggeration, but it would never feel that way to Arlie. If not for her, Brett may still be alive. As if she were reading her mind, Meaghan put her hand to the glass of the door. "Arlie, open up, please. I need to talk to you."

Against her better judgement, Arlie pulled open the door. "What?" she asked, not bothering to hide the venom in her voice. "What do you want?"

"I know..." she said, her eyes bloodshot, hair a mess. It was the first time Arlie had seen her looking less than perfect. "I know I have no right to be here." She smelled of bourbon and cigarettes, and it didn't look like she'd changed clothes in several days.

"You're right about that."

"It's just...it's just that I-I miss him so much."

Arlie closed her eyes as if she'd been slapped. "You have no right to miss him, Meaghan. He was never yours to miss."

"I know," she said, openly sobbing. "But I do. I loved him so much. I know you must hate me. I don't blame you for that...but I loved him. I loved him like you did and—."

"Do," Arlie corrected her.

"Excuse me?"

"Loved him like I do. Brett was my husband, and despite his flaws, I still love him. That's my right as his wife. You were nothing but a fling." She said the words, though she knew they weren't true. Flings don't last years. Flings don't contain the words 'I love you.'

"That's not..." She covered her mouth, and for a second Arlie thought she may get sick. Instead, she lowered her hand. "That's not true. I was not a fling to him. He loved me. I know he loved you, too. I would never deny that. But he did love me, Arlie. He loved us both. Maybe in different ways. Maybe on different levels. But he did love me."

Arlie locked her jaw, narrowing her eyes at Meaghan. "What do you want, Meaghan? Why did you come here?"

"I just...I know you must hate me, but we miss him the same way. I thought we could stick together somehow." She held out a hand for Arlie, who jerked away as if she were on fire.

"Excuse me?"

"Don't you see? We're the only ones hurting this way. We need each other."

"No," Arlie spat. "No. We aren't the only ones hurting. Brett's family is hurting. His parents. His brother. So many people are hurting over his loss."

"But not the same way we are."

"We are not the same, you and me," Arlie said, moving her hand—finger pointed—back and forth between their chests. "We aren't. Just because we loved the same man, that doesn't make us equal. He may have made a bed with both of us, but I was his wife. We made a vow to each other. We spent twelve years by each other's side. That could never compare to what you had. Never. You aren't equal to me, Meaghan. Even if he did love you. He could never love you like he loved me."

"You don't know that."

"You need to leave now," Arlie said, stepping back to shut the door.

Meaghan placed her foot out to stop it. "Arlie, you don't have to like me, but you need to talk to me. I need to get what I deserve out of this—"

"What you deserve?" Arlie seethed, spit foaming in the corners of her mouth. "What you deserve, Meaghan? What is that exactly?"

"I just—"

"Because let me tell you what I deserve. I deserve a husband who doesn't lie to me. I deserve a husband who actually meant the vows he made to me. A husband who doesn't stray at the first girl with a low-cut blouse and an even lower IQ. But more than that, I deserve a husband who's alive. Thanks to you, I will

111

never have any of those things. As far as I'm concerned, you're the reason he's dead."

Meaghan took a step back as if she'd been punched, a hand to her chest. She bent over at the waist, taking a deep breath as her gaze seared into Arlie's. "You don't mean that."

"I do," she said firmly. "I do mean that, Meaghan. And I hope that sticks with you. I hope those words, that horrible truth eats into you every day of the rest of your miserable life. You are the reason Brett is gone. Not me. We will never...never...be even."

"I should've gotten some of his life insurance," Meaghan shouted as Arlie moved to shut the door.

"Excuse me?" She pushed the door back open, a new fireball of anger in her belly.

"I have expenses. Brett had been taking care of me. He was helping me with my bills. Since he's been gone...I'm behind on everything. He promised to take care of me."

"If you think you are entitled to one cent of my money, you're insane. Don't you have a husband? Why on earth did you need mine?"

"My husband is never here," she cried, her head in her palms. "He won't be home for another year and a half, and when he does come home, he won't recognize this...this shell of a woman he left behind."

"What do you mean?"

She shrugged her shoulders, tears still cascading down her red cheeks. "He's deployed."

"You mean to tell me your husband is in the military, and you are cheating on him with a married man?" She curled her lip in disgust. This woman was everything wrong with the world. "You told Brett he was at work the night we had dinner."

"That wasn't technically a lie," she said, her voice a squeak.

"He's always at work. And it's not like we planned it." She cried again. *"I loved my husband. But, you have no idea what it's like, having to be away from the man you love."*

"Yes, actually I do, Meaghan. You made sure of that."

"It wasn't my fault," Meaghan screamed, lunging at her. Her actions caught Arlie off guard, and she jumped back. Meaghan's weight landed on her, pushing her inside the house to the living room floor. She cried out, trying desperately to shove the girl off of her. Meaghan was dead weight, her sobs rippling through her body. Arlie wasn't sure if it was anger or sadness causing her tears. She pummelled her arms into Arlie's chest, soft, baby-like punches that did no real damage. Arlie pushed her off, finally relieving herself of the weight.

"Get off of me, Meaghan."

"He loved me," Meaghan screamed, grabbing onto Arlie's legs as she tried to stand.

"I said get off," she repeated, anger coursing through her.

"I know you don't believe me, Arlie, but he did. He did love me. And I loved him. He meant everything to—"

Arlie shoved her knee into the girl's face, trying to get her to let go as the venom worked its way through her body. She watched in slow motion as Meaghan's head flopped back, crashing into the corner of the coffee table with a loud CRACK.

The girl crumpled to the floor, her body in an uncomfortable position, but she didn't move. *"Meaghan?"* Arlie called, her voice soft. It was no use. Like a light, the girl was out. Gone. Dead.

She took a step back, collapsing inches from the body and letting her own tears finally begin to release.

CHAPTER TWENTY-FOUR

J ust a year and a half after Arlie had buried Meaghan in
the backyard, another knock sounded at the door. This
time, it was a face she didn't recognize at all. He was
dressed in jeans and a T-shirt, his dark hair neatly cut with
sharp, recently done edges. She opened the door cautiously. In
the back of her mind, she had been waiting for this day, the day
her crime would finally come to light.

She opened the door, trying to keep her face unreadable.
"Hello?"

"Hi," he said cautiously, "I'm sorry to bother you. I just...um,
my name is Alec Hopewood. I think you know my wife."

"Your wife?" she asked, trying to calm the nerves that were
causing her heart to flutter.

"Her name is Meaghan. She's missing."

"Missing?" Her voice was shaking, and she prayed he
wouldn't notice.

"Yeah. I'm sorry, could I come in? It's just...it's a really long
story."

She nodded without conscious thought. "S-sure."

"Thanks," he said, his dark eyes burning into hers. He walked into the small living room, sticking his hands in his pockets. He had the stature of someone in the military, his shoulders square, gait even. "I know this is kind of crazy."

"What exactly are you hoping I'll be able to help you with?"

"I don't know...exactly. You see, I was deployed up until recently. My wife stopped answering my calls about a year ago. We lost contact, and I believed she had left me."

"Were you two having problems?" she asked, though as soon as the question left her lips she regretted it. What business was that of hers?

He sighed. "Things hadn't been...good, for a long time. Actually, I thought she may have been having an affair. But, when I came home...my house was...it's like she just walked out the door without a word. Her purse and phone are missing, but all of the food was spoiled. The post office has been holding and returning our mail because our box was so full. It's as if...as if she were planning on returning but never did."

"Is it possible she left you for the man she was having an affair with?"

He lowered his brow, seemingly taken aback by her question. "It's possible, yes. But, no money has come out of our account. The deposits go in, our bills come out automatically, but she's spent no money in the past year and a half. I called her job, and they said she stopped coming in altogether around that time. They thought she was depressed after the shooting."

"Was she?"

His jaw was tight. "I don't...I don't know, honestly. I wish I did. I hadn't talked to her in so long."

"So, why is it you think I can help you? Did I know your wife?"

"I'm hoping so," he said, pulling out his cellphone and

holding out a picture of Meaghan. Her smile was endearing, yet her eyes looked as though they held a secret. Arlie's secret. It was as if she were begging her to admit what she'd done. "Her name is Meaghan Hopewood. And I believe...I believe she worked with your husband. I found...I found messages between the two of them on her computer. They were close, I think."

She pretended to stare at the picture, though her gaze grew fuzzy. "I don't...maybe. I mean, I think I heard him mention her name once or twice." She felt cool tears filling her eyes.

"I'm sorry. I know your husband passed away. I'm so sorry for your loss."

"Thank you," she said, biting her lip and looking down.

"I just...I hoped, maybe...after the shooting, I don't know what happened. She just, changed. I don't know how to explain it. I'd hoped you might know something that could help me find her."

Okay, so he didn't know anything. He wasn't suspicious. She let out a breath. "I'm sorry. I don't."

He pinched the bridge of his nose. "That's okay, it's not your fault."

She nodded. "I do hope you find her."

He frowned. "Thank you. I'll be going to the police next. Hopefully they can help." He started to turn around, but stopped, his gaze dancing over her face. "Did you...did you know anything about their relationship? Meaghan and your husband?" She tried to keep her face stony, though it must have faltered because his expression suddenly told her he knew her secrets. "You did, didn't you?"

"I don't know what you're talking about."

"I think you do," he said, taking an angry step toward her. "I think you know exactly what I'm talking about, Ms. Montgomery. Like I said, I found messages on the computer.

Messages between her and your husband. Messages between you and her."

"Me and her? I never messaged your wife."

"Yeah," he said firmly. "You did. Maybe you didn't know it was her. She was using the name Roosevelt."

Arlie gasped, truly shocked. Roosevelt. Her stalker. Those messages had started so long before she found out about the affair. Brett had lied to her when he'd said it had only been going on for a month. She swallowed, looking back at Alec.

"The messages she sent you, begging you to leave your husband. It was sick. I'm sorry for that. Meaghan was...lonely. She'd never done well on her own. It doesn't justify what she did, but she wasn't a bad person."

She shook her head, looking down. "You should go."

"Fine," he said firmly. "I'll go. But I'll be back with the police. If you won't talk to me, maybe you'll talk to them." He turned, reaching for the door. Thinking quickly, Arlie grabbed the small cast iron skillet that held a decorative candle from her coffee table. She lifted it above his head, bringing it down with full force just as he pulled the door open.

His body crumpled quickly, the blood pooling from his head in an instant. Now, what was she going to do with him?

CHAPTER TWENTY-FIVE

PRESENT DAY

After it was all said and done, Arlie dumped the body in a field on the outskirts of town. She'd bought a construction vest and placed it on him, thinking that if he was found, people would assume he'd died doing construction work. Mine work. Something. Anything that wouldn't point to their connection. She took his wallet, leaving him nothing to be identified with. So, you can imagine her surprise when she was driving back into town from a quick trip to Arbordale the next day and spied the man she'd murdered...walking through the fields and headed straight for Crimson Falls.

When she'd pulled over, she'd been trying to decide what to do. But he looked confused. Genuinely confused. And when he approached her car, he hadn't recognized her. He'd asked who she was. Where he was. He didn't remember what she'd done. He didn't remember anything.

And so, Arlie saw her second chance. But just to be safe, she kept him close. If his memory came back, she wasn't sure what she'd do, but she'd have to get rid of him. And not in the garden, she didn't need any more damning evidence around her home.

But, she'd grown to like Mason. Honestly, she had. None of it was personal. She'd done what she had to. She'd started the Bartholomew Danger blog as a way to test out a pen name when her publisher had been forceful about the idea. But, since the success had happened with her legal name, she'd forgotten about it. Until now. Until it became useful again.

The murders, the blogging…she'd done it because her sales were dwindling and her writing had taken a turn for the worst since Brett's passing. She couldn't bring herself to churn out any new books. But in a moment of weakness, she'd turned to what made her famous in the first place. Death. Tragedy. And it had been proven to work again.

It was a pure whim that made her commit the first murder. Perry was easy enough. She never knew if it would work. When the police didn't immediately connect her books to it, she committed the second, and then the third. And then, when too many eyes were on her, she'd made it look like someone had attacked her. The final piece of the puzzle her books had laid out. The writer had to die. Only, she wasn't that crazy. She wasn't going to kill herself. Just make it look like someone had tried. Granted, in the book the writer had been poisoned, but she'd had to improvise and no one seemed to mind. It had taken every bit of her strength and bravery to shove her own face into that counter top. And oh, how it had hurt. If she hadn't had the adrenaline coursing through her from the chief's phone call, she might have chickened out.

In the end, it was Mason's own offer that had made him the obvious scapegoat. She'd never planned to point the finger at him. She'd hoped for a life with him, actually. They were both wronged in Meaghan and Brett's affair. They deserved happiness. In the beginning, she knew she had to keep him close, to make sure his memory never came back, but she'd begun to fall for him.

And then she stopped herself. Love was what had broken her heart in the first place. Loving a man, a living, breathing man who could stop living and breathing at any moment, had caused her to experience the greatest heart-break of her life. And she couldn't experience that again. She wouldn't survive it.

So, when Mason had said he'd do anything to protect her, that he owed her everything...he had sealed his fate. Arlie had placed the murder weapons in his room, along with the wallet she'd taken from his pocket when she'd dumped the body, and sent the email knowing the IP address would show her house, because the blogs were posted from her computer. In fact, it was funny that she'd chosen to use the desktop to post the final blog. Some-how, she subconsciously must've known it might come to this. When Brett had hidden her laptop's IP address years ago, it was to guarantee her anonymity if either her pen name or legal name ever made it big, but in the end it had been the thing to save her. Brett had saved her. But so had Mason.

She set him up, not because she didn't care about him, but because she cared too much. She couldn't allow herself to do that again.

And now it was over. Mason was locked up, and no one would believe him even if his memory did come back.

She was free. Her books were viral once again. Her heart was still broken, but that was healing.

Everything was going to be better.

And she deserved better, didn't she?

As she stood at her husband's graveside, she laid the bouquet of flowers down, wiping away a quick tear. She still loved him. There was a giant rift inside of her, threatening to destroy her sanity. Her heart, her brain. They were split, in a constant war. One huge part of her was so wrapped up in loving him, while the other would despise him for the rest of her life. It was funny, the way she thought of him. Despite his many flaws, she loved Brett with every fiber of her being. If he were still alive, she would've taken him back. Her heart ached for him. That was one side of her. The other side, the one that was partially glad the choice to take him back had been ripped away from her, was furious with him. And she wasn't sure that would ever go away. Her husband, as much as he'd loved her, had made bad choices. He'd done horrible things to their marriage, and in the end, those things had cost him his life. Sure, the actual affair had little to do with the gunman, but Brett wouldn't have jumped in front of the bullet to save the janitor. He did it for Meaghan. He'd died for her, and then she'd died for him. At the hands of his wife.

And Meaghan's husband would help make Brett's wife famous, again.

It was poetic, really.

Arlie liked poetry.

She loved Brett.

She missed Brett.

She hated Brett.

She'd kill for Brett.

She'd die for Brett.

Brett would die for Meaghan.

Had died for Meaghan.

Brett had given her a happy life. Until he hadn't. In the end, he'd ruined her life. His death had started the chain of events that gave her everything she'd ever wanted from her career, but also made her into the monster she was today.

As she walked away from his grave, she thought about the book she'd started writing a few months ago, the one starring Mason Beaumont. *The Monster Within*. A book about a writer who was stalked by a man who would use her books as a murder plan in hopes to grow close to her. It would be fabulous. Phoebe would love it. Fans would eat it up. She liked to think somewhere, Brett was watching her, enjoying the show. He'd helped to inspire it, after all.

She guessed she'd been right about him. Even in death, Brett was the only one who could get her to write.

Through death, she'd learned to love. In tragedy, she'd found success. Arlie was the pure definition of irony, and from now on, she was going to embrace that.

THE CRIMSON FALLS NOVELLA SERIES

READ ALL EIGHT:
Original Sin by Greta Cribbs
The Last Dupont by Rachel Renee
All the Dark Corners by Emerald O'Brien
Flawed Plan by Amabel Daniels
Returned Home by Julie Strier
Sight in the Dark by AM Ialacci
The Stranger in the Woods by Kiersten Modglin
Little Girl Lost by Laurèn Lee

Join the Crimson Falls Reader Group on Facebook for more behind the scenes details, exclusive information, and a community to discuss all the novellas in: https://www.facebook.com/groups/CrimsonFallsReaderGroup/

ACKNOWLEDGEMENTS

Thank you so much for reading my contribution to the Crimson Falls Novella Series, The Stranger in the Woods. I truly hope you enjoyed this story and had a few surprises along the way.

As always, this book would not be possible without the help of so many people and I need to give them all special thanks.

First and foremost, to my husband and little girl—I love you both so much. Thank you for always encouraging me and believing in my dreams, no matter how crazy they may seem.

To the rest of my crazy family: Mom, Dad, Kaitie, Kortnee, Kyleigh, Granny, and Papa, Nan, and Pop, Uncle Tommy, and way too many aunts, uncles, and cousins to mention—thank you for reading my stories long before they were good and always believing this day would come.

To my Crimson Crew: Emerald, Laurèn, Rachel, Greta, A.M., Julie, and Amabel—I had so much fun with you ladies creating this creepy little town. Thank you for your brilliant minds. I consider myself lucky to get to work with you all.

To my editor, Sarah West—thank you for always giving me amazing insight and suggestions. I'm so glad to have you as a part of my team!

To my cover designer, Alora Kate—your designs never fail to amaze me. Thank you for your unending patience and creativity!

To my PR team at Enticing Journey—thank you guys for working so hard to get this book in front of new readers! You guys are the best!

To my Twisted Readers, Street Team, and Review Team—thank you, thank you, thank you! I've said it before but I'll say it again: you guys keep me going. I couldn't do this without all of the love and support you show me and my stories. I love you!

And finally, to you—thank you for taking a chance on me. Whether you are a brand new reader or one who's been with me for the long haul, I can't thank you enough for supporting me. There was once a point in time when I wished for you...I wished that someone, anyone, would read my stories and love them like I do. I hope that's the case. If this is your first time reading my books, I sincerely hope you'll hurry to check out the rest of my work. If you're a returning reader, thank you for continuing to believe in me! I couldn't be here without you.

From the bottom of my slightly cold, full of dangerous plot twists heart, *thank you.*

P.S. If you want to help me out even more, please consider leaving a review on this book. More reviews mean more visibility for my books, and your review could be the thing that convinces a skeptical reader to take a chance on me. It doesn't have to be long, just a few sentences will do. If you'd like to leave a review, just click here. Either way, thank you again for reading!

ABOUT THE AUTHOR

Kiersten Modglin is a suspense author who enjoys dabbling in all the sub-genres. A Netflix addict, Shonda Rhimes super-fan, psychology fanatic, and indoor enthusiast, Kiersten enjoys rainy days spent with her nose in a book. More than anything, she loves reading & creating life-changing stories.

Sign up for Kiersten's newsletter here:
http://eepurl.com/b3cNFP
Readers's Group:
www.facebook.com/groups/kierstenstwistedreaders

www.kierstenmodglinauthor.com
Facebook
Twitter

Instagram
Goodreads
BookBub
Amazon
YouTube

ALSO BY KIERSTEN MODGLIN

STANDALONE NOVELS

Becoming Mrs. Abbott

The List

The Missing Piece

Playing Jenna

The Beginning After

The Good Neighbors

The Better Choice

THE MESSES SERIES

The Cleaner (The Messes, #1)

The Healer (The Messes, #2)

The Liar (The Messes, #3)

The Prisoner (The Messes, #4)

NOVELLAS

The Long Route: A Lover's Landing Novella